S. Howard Taylor

Kate Byrne

A Novel: Vol. II.

S. Howard Taylor

Kate Byrne
A Novel: Vol. II.

ISBN/EAN: 9783337031695

Printed in Europe, USA, Canada, Australia, Japan

Cover: Foto ©Andreas Hilbeck / pixelio.de

More available books at **www.hansebooks.com**

KATE BYRNE.

A Novel.

BY

S. HOWARD-TAYLOR.

IN TWO VOLUMES.
VOL. II.

London:
SAMUEL TINSLEY,
10, SOUTHAMPTON STREET, STRAND.

1874.

KATE BYRNE.

CHAPTER I.

ADY DENTON filled her house with guests, coming and going, for some weeks. The gentlemen amused themselves a good deal out of doors, smoked, played billiards, rode, hunted, and made themselves between times agreeable to the ladies of the party. They thought that Lord Denton was very much altered, and a very lucky fellow; that the old place was wonderfully improved, and vastly more comfortable, through having a mistress. The ladies all

agreed that Lady Denton did her duties as
hostess wonderfully well and easily; each
day's arrangements were made agreeable to
almost every one, the evenings were always
pleasant and lively, Lady Denton doing
her best to make every one at home. No
one would have thought that she was only
in her first year of married life, and that
it was her first experience of seeing guests
alone. She had had her aunt in London,
and of course in her own home she had
not taken the management out of Miss
Casteldi's hands when she returned from
school, but had been only too glad to have
nothing to do with it. No difficulty had
presented itself to Kate's mind. She knew
what she *ought* to do, and did it, simply
and naturally, and successfully, as it turned
out; she had determined to fill her house,
and while helping to amuse others, enjoy
herself, assuring Helen, who of course was
in her confidence, " that a number of people

were far less trouble than a few; they are not so likely to clash or to be bored with each other, if there are enough to prevent the necessity of talking to the same person every day."

One evening Kate had been singing a duet with one of the gentlemen, and had got up from the piano, and was standing carelessly against it, talking and laughing with several others who had been listening to them. An elderly lady, who was snugly ensconced in the corner of a luxurious sofa at the end of the room, looked very much as if she would have liked to indulge in a short nap, but in reality she was watching Kate narrowly. Presently Mary Clenning came and sat down on the same sofa, and was asked in an under-tone "if she did not think Lady Denton seemed at no loss to entertain her visitors? It was quite wonderful, if one remembered it was her first year, wasn't it?"

"Not to us," replied Mary. "We always knew Lady Denton would make an excellent mistress of Denton Court. I always envied her the power she has of making all things bend to her superior will."

"Oh, I see you knew her before she was married, indeed. Do you come from Ireland too?"

"No! we live not very far from here, and saw a good deal of her when she came to visit our neighbours the Leighs; in fact, it was at our house that Lord Denton met her, a little more than a year ago, when my brother came of age," replied Mary.

"Ah, indeed! how interesting, to be sure. They had a very short engagement, I know. Do you think they are well matched and happy? I see so little of them together, that I can barely judge for myself."

"Oh, of course they are," replied Mary, warmly. "There is not the shadow of a doubt that they are. How could it be otherwise ? She is so young and handsome, there is not a woman in the whole county to be compared to her, my papa says."

"Ah, my dear girl, I can quite remember the time when I was as enthusiastic as you are over my friends. Every one that I *wished* to be happy I made happy in my own mind; but as you get older you get wiser, and see things in a different light. And one loses all the younger fancies that satisfy one so easily; and one's common-sense comes a little more into use with advancing years, I assure you," said the lady.

"Indeed," replied Mary, tartly. "I cannot see, though, what that has to do with our subject. For my part, I shall make a point of declining to use my common-sense at all, if I have any, and shall retain the girlish feeling when I get older, which I suppose I must do like the rest of people, even if I have to get gloomy."

Mrs. Clenning came up at that moment, and Mary rose to give her her seat, glad to get away from her not very pleasant companion; and as she went away, she could but hope that her mother would be able to get on better than she had. Mrs. Clenning was certainly not an improvement upon her daughter, for she began to pour out her hopes and fears (or rather fears only, for she had no hopes) into the old lady's ear, so that before long she began to yawn, and made an excuse for moving to another part of the room, and went to join her own daughter, a tall, plain, but not young person.

In days gone by, this same young lady (as she was still called by some, and certainly was thought so by herself and mother,) had had designs, which, if she could have carried them into effect, would have made her mistress of the house in which they were now visiting. She greeted her mother with the following remark, made in a low tone,

as she appeared to show her an elegant piece
of fancy work she had just finished,—

" Did you ever see such a dreadful flirt as
Lady Denton is ? What a fool Denton was
to marry her. She will ruin him or break
his heart in a few years, or I am very much
mistaken."

" She may do the latter, I dare say, easily
enough, for I can see he is desperately fond
of her ; but as to ruin, what with his wealth
and her own, a little extravagance cannot
matter very much, I should think."

Had Lady Denton been older and not
quite so good looking, it is just possible the
above-mentioned ladies would have found
more to admire in her—at least, the younger
one might have.

A plain woman is generally more kindly
disposed to those to whom Nature has not
been more lavish of good looks than to herself.
Much has been said about the spite and
envy of beautiful women to each other ; this

is undoubtedly true, but it cannot be compared to the deep hatred and aversion felt
towards them by those who are plain and
uninteresting, especially when the latter are
no longer young. No one can be more
spiteful, harder, more eager to catch at and
make the most of any little fault or weak-
ness of a beautiful fellow-sister, than the
woman who has all her life longed for
the attention and admiration she has seen
so freely lavished upon those favourites of
society—beauties.

Of course, these remarks can and do only
apply to those weak, narrow-minded fol-
lowers of fashion who waste half their time
and all the sense they have over their per-
sonal appearance, and never get rewarded
for their pains. It does not necessarily
follow that, because a girl is plain she must
be slighted and treated coldly; on the
contrary, if she has a cultivated mind and
nice manners, she, in all probability, will be

as much sought after and really more appreciated than many a beautiful girl is.

When Kate was once again without visitors, she found herself obliged to rest and keep quiet, and she very unwillingly had to refuse her father's pressing invitation to come and spend the Christmas and New Year with him. They hoped to persuade him to come to them instead, but he could not undertake the journey in such cold weather.

One evening, almost immediately after dinner, Kate was sitting alone, when all at once, without any warning, she fainted away. Fortunately, a man-servant just came in, and rushed for his master and Norah. Lord Denton was dreadfully alarmed. At first he thought she was dead; then he saw she breathed, and held her in his arms, while the faithful Norah used her best endeavours to bring her beloved mistress back to consciousness. Kate opened her eyes and

sighed heavily, then silent tears came slowly
down her checks, and in reply to her husband's earnest inquiry she assured them she
was quite well. As soon as Lord Denton
heard the sound of her voice he was himself
again. Leaving Kate to Norah's care, he
left the room, and despatched a man-servant
with a hurriedly-written note to Dr. Andrews,
asking him to come immediately to the
Court. He then returned to Kate, and knelt
down by the sofa on which she was resting.
She held out her hand to him, and smiled
faintly. "Oh, my dear, sweet Kitty," he
said, "I am so relieved to see you better.
Coward that I am, I could not exist one single
moment without knowing you were sharing
that existence."

Kate's closed eyes and pale face told him
he must not say too much to her just now,
however much he longed to pour into her
ear all the endearing words which came so
readily at that moment; and Norah wisely

. suggested she had better be kept perfectly quiet till the doctor came. As the last-named gentleman lived quite three miles from Denton, it was some time before he made an appearance, although he started immediately after receiving the letter. He found Lady Denton quite recovered, though still on the sofa. He felt her pulse, asked some questions, then said that there was no cause for anxiety.

"Oh, I dare say not, Dr. Andrews," replied Kate. "I did not know Lord Denton had sent for you till after the man was gone. It is, however, the first time I ever fainted, and I confess I was a little startled myself. I have not felt quite the thing for some days, but I thought it would pass over if I tried not to think about it."

"Yes; a good night's rest is all you require. I will come over though early to-morrow. You are a little nervous; keep

quiet, and go to bed at once," replied **Dr.
Andrews.**

Lord Denton was waiting for him in a
state of great anxiety, and was delighted to
hear the doctor say that there was nothing
alarming the matter with his wife. "Just
a passing faint, which was not an unusual
thing when people were not very strong,"
he said, as he shook hands, and promised
to come the next day.

This was a piece of good fortune for Dr.
Andrews. He worked very hard, and had very
little pay—so little, that sometimes, in spite
of the economy his nice little wife always
practised, he found, or perhaps one should
say, they found, it almost impossible to make
both ends meet. They had six very small
children to clothe, feed, and care for; besides which, an invalid sister of Mrs. Andrews
had lived for some years with them, and was
almost entirely dependent on them. To his
wife's credit, be it said, she never once mur-

mured even to her husband at the fresh cares-
this gave her, and the extra work for her
already full hands to do. She knew they
could not afford to keep another servant
now, whatever they may have thought of
doing before, so she quietly worked on, and
managed as well as ever. The children became very fond of auntie, and, with all its
trials and pinchings, Dr. Andrews's home was
perhaps as happy a one as could be found
anywhere. When Lord Denton married,
Mrs. Andrews had hoped that perhaps her
husband would be chosen for their medical
man when the family were at the Court;
but of course there were others about as near
in point of distance who had equal chance of
being called in, though none of them were
more clever or greater favourites than her
husband, she thought. So the loving little
woman waited anxiously for his return from
the Court, and, after hearing how Lady Denton was, asked if she had been nice to him.

"Oh, yes; perfectly friendly and charming, my dear. We are old friends, you know. I saw a good deal of her when she was laid up with a sprain at The Ridgway."

"Of course, I know that, Henry; but then she was only plain Kate Byrne, and rather proud too, I fancied; so I did not know if she would be still more so now she is Lady Denton," said Mrs. Andrews.

"That's a mistake, my dear. She is just as nice as ever she was, I assure you; but as they have sent for me, you will, of course, be seeing something of her by-and-by, so don't come to any conclusions until you see for yourself."

"I hope they are very happy," replied Mrs. Andrews, "and that Lord Denton intends to settle down into an attentive husband and a good landlord."

"Of course he will," said the Doctor. "Does he not dote on the very ground she walks on? A man when he marries at his age generally makes a thoroughly good husband, my dear, especially if he has been what people call wild beforehand. I dare say she is entirely master and mistress too."

"I hope so, with all my heart, for I am positive that he is in greater need of some one to hold the reins over him than most men are. There are a few in this world, I suppose, who can be left to themselves, and come to no harm, but Lord Denton is not one of them," replied Mrs. Andrews.

"Well, my dear, I don't wish to contradict you; you are, I know, a clever little woman, but I am uncommonly tired, so, if you have no objection, we will retire, as I must be off early to-morrow morning. Some sleep will do me more good than listening to scandal about our neighbours."

When Dr. Andrews called at the Court the next morning, he found Kate had re-gained her spirits wonderfully. He stayed

some time with her, and they chatted about
their own affairs to each other,—Kate going
over the time when he attended her last, and
he, in reply to her questions, telling her about
his children, and the invalid sister. Kate
was so sorry to hear how much she suffered.
She had heard of her, she said, but had no
idea that she was never able to leave her
· couch, and she said that she would certainly
call to see her soon, and take some books
from the library. Lord Denton begged him
to call again in a few days, as Lady Denton
liked the change of seeing and talking to
him.

When he returned home late that day, he
found his wife in great spirits. A parcel
of books had come from the Court with Lady
Denton's compliments, and a nice little note,
in which Lady Denton begged that Mrs.
Andrews would send them, and get them
changed as often as her sister wished. Kate's
kind nature had prompted her to show this

little attention to the invalid, as the doctor had said she liked reading better than anything else. But this was only the beginning of her kindnesses, which went on all through the winter, and took a more substantial shape than the merely lending a few interesting books.

CHAPTER II.

ABOUT the middle of the month of February of the next year, silence and sadness and death reigned in Denton Court. Light footsteps moved noiselessly to and fro in the soft-carpeted rooms, and every one spoke in whispers, both up and down stairs. The long drive from the lodge to the house was covered with thick straw to deaden the slightest sound, and even the dogs had all been moved away to the farm, so that their noise might not be heard in the house. Kate lies faint and ill in her own darkened room; the delirium of the last two or three days has almost ex-

hausted her ; she is perfectly calm and quiet
now, dreamy and unconscious; loving hearts
and hands are near her, Miss Casteldi and
Helen Leigh, anticipating and attending her
every want with sad foreboding and dread.
A tiny baby form is motionless and still, like
a beautiful marble image, on a pure white
bed in a chamber near its mother, who had
so nearly lost her life after giving it birth.
Sweet wee thing! it had only had three days
of suffering life granted it; but Kate had
had it near her, and feasted her loving eyes
and mother's heart over it, framing happy
thoughts of future hopes; then she became
too ill to see or know it. Every one bowed
submissively to the merciful will which took
it away from its pain, the anxiety which
was felt for Kate's life and reason almost
preventing grief for the little sufferer.

Lord Denton had been like one distracted.
He hovered about the passages round Kate's
room, almost wearying every one with his

constant questions about her. He had sent off to London for a skilful man he knew there, who had been staying a day or two in the house; he was, however, obliged to return to some other patient, and had persuaded Lord Denton, for a change, to drive down to the railway with him.

" I will come in a day or two," he said, as they drove along. " The worst is over ; with great care and good nursing Lady Denton will recover. You may place every confidence in Andrews. I can see with half an eye that he is clever and reliable, and knows what his patient requires."

This of course comforted the anxious husband a good deal, and he tried to make himself believe that his worst fears would not now be realized. He had been denied admission to Kate's room, but one evening, when she had somewhat improved, he begged so hard to be allowed to see her for a few moments, that Dr. Andrews found it impossible to resist any longer. Kate had never once asked either for him or her baby. She knew her aunt and every one about her perfectly well, but did not appear to care to talk or to be talked to. A stout, comfortable person, with a handsome soft cap on her head, moved silently away from the side of the bed as Lord Denton approached, and knelt down by Kate, who was lying near the edge. She looked pleased to see him, and held out her hand, which he took and kissed again and again. "My darling, my darling!" he whispered tenderly, as he bent his head to hers, his whole frame convulsed with his combined grief and thankfulness.

Kate put her hand on his head, and told him not to grieve. Large tears stole down her cheeks as she passed her delicate fingers through his hair, treating him like a little child, so surprised was she to see him feeling her illness so deeply. Neither of them spoke for a few moments; then Lord

Denton got up from his knees, and said softly,—

"Oh, Kate, my precious wife! I have been so intensely miserable all this time."

"But I am better now," Kate answered, as she raised her eyes, very subdued and languid, but more loving than they had ever before been to him. "You must not grieve any more."

"No, of course not, my darling! You are sure to get well. I am full of hope and love for you, and, oh, so happy for this glimpse of you. It was so cruel of them to keep me away," replied her husband.

How quickly the moments flew, and how delightful it was for him to be able to tell Kate over again how much he loved her, and for her to listen patiently and look pleased to hear him. But nurse found that too much talking was going on, so she came and beckoned him away, he reluctantly following her, walking backwards on tiptoe, so as

not to lose for a moment the sight of the
sweet pale face which was smiling him good-
bye.

Lady Denton gained strength after this
very quickly, and when she was able to leave
her room, Lord Denton carried her up and
down stairs, in and out of the house and
carriage, not allowing the willing servants
to do the slightest thing for her that he
could possibly do himself. Every little wish,
want, or whim was gratified almost before it
was expressed; and Kate constantly assured
both her aunt and her husband, with a touch
of the old girlish animation, that they were
doing their best to make her more spoilt than
ever. As soon as she was able to bear the
journey, they took her home to her father.
She wished to go there more than to any of
the places suggested to her for change of air,
and her medical advisers thought that, upon
the whole, nothing would do her more good.
As far as her husband's wishes on the subject

went, Kate had given little thought or consideration. He had wanted to take her to
the South of France, but she hated travelling
so far, she said; and although he suggested
several other fresh places that would have
done as well, and where he could have had her
more to himself, he had to give way when
he found she was bent upon paying her father
a visit, and especially as no objection was
raised to her doing so by her doctors. But
he felt that he would see so much less of her
there, and that there would be an end to his
many little delicate attentions, which had
given him so much pleasure to show her.

But of course this was selfish, he thought
upon reflection; Kate could not go on for
ever being an invalid and treated as one.
Instead of dreaming of such a possibility,
he ought to be thankful she was so far well,
which indeed he was; but still, in spite of
all the anxiety and care he had had, the last
few months had been the happiest in his

married life. It was a great pleasure to Kate to be in her old home once again; how glad she was to see her father,—he looked so well, she thought; and they fell back, as it were, into the old days quite naturally,—rides or drives in the mornings, visiting after luncheon, and cards and music in the evenings.

Kate got strong and well as ever. Every one complimented her upon the improvement her native air had made in her; and she showed decided reluctance to leave Ireland whenever her husband mentioned taking her to London. She had, with her renewed health, returned to her old way of opposing what he wanted to do, and as it was the most difficult thing in the world for him, alas! to say "No" to her (or to any one else that he cared for, by the way), especially since her illness, he had quietly to submit to be tyrannized over, and stay his wife's pleasure. However, they made a short visit, quite at the end of the season, for a few

operas, and the pictures. Her portrait at
the Academy had attracted universal admiration; it was well done and well hung. She
was sitting at a small table, arranging flowers
in a glass basket, and looked very natural
and life-like, in a plain white muslin morning
gown and bright ribbons. Although a great
many of their friends and acquaintances had
left London, Kate found plenty of amusement and admirers, and, as might be expected after so long an absence, her husband's
time was fully occupied.

.They were on the eve of leaving for St.
Leonards, when a telegram reached them
from Aunt Neta, to say that they must come
at once, as Mr. Byrne was dangerously ill.
Kate had just returned from her morning
ride, and was almost stunned with the
news. Fortunately, her husband came in to
luncheon, and persuaded her to stay quietly
in her room till it was time to go to the
station. She had given orders for the car-

riage to come round far too early, and was in a state of feverish impatience to be gone.

"Did ever any one have such trouble?" she exclaimed, as she paced about her bed-room, looking for the hundredth time at her tiny watch, which seemed scarcely to move a minute, her mind full of all the sad misgivings we all feel under such painful circumstances. Lord Denton and Norah did their best to soothe her, and as they drove to the station, he suggested all the most sanguine and hopeful views he could imagine. But she scarcely heard or heeded him, and except to remark that they were driving so slowly, or to entreat him to get her home as quickly as possible, she hardly said a single sentence all the way. Of course, she anticipated the worst, and blamed herself again and again for leaving home when she did. "I should have stayed a little longer with my dear father," she mentally ex-claimed, as she sat on the deck of the steamer. "Poor darling! how he has longed for me. I know he loves me better than any one else in this world. Perhaps he is not as ill as Aunt Neta thinks he is; she was always nervous about him. I will soon nurse him back to his old self again if— Ah! if. Would they never get there?" she said to her husband, who assured her that a few minutes more would see them landed.

As they neared the house Kate grew paler, and leaned back in the carriage, as if fearing to catch the first sight of the steps where her father had so often stood to welcome her home, and where she had seen him last. They found the blinds down, and knew that all their haste had been in vain; and Miss Casteldi, who came out to meet them, burst into bitter tears as soon as Kate spoke to her. Mr. Byrne had had a kind of fit, from which he never rallied, dying without regaining his senses, or saying one sensible word. He was almost gone when the telegram had been sent off; but Miss Casteldi was afraid of alarming Kate by saying more than she did, as she knew they would come as quickly as possible.

Lord Denton was terribly upset and grieved, and Kate's stony, pale face made him anxious about her. It seemed so unnatural to him her not crying, and he found it so difficult to say anything to comfort her. He went with her to the quiet room where her father lay, and uncovered the still, cold face, on which there was no trace of suffering. A few white hairs had been tenderly smoothed over the brow, and but for the solemn stillness he might have been sleeping only. Those who have passed through the same heavy trial, and been too late to have one look or one word from the loved one's lips, will understand what Kate's feelings were, as she stood there, with throbbing heart and tearless eye, passing her hand over the loved face, and kissing the cold hands.

Death is always solemn and depressing whenever it claims any of our dear ones, young or old. However long we have watched and waited, hoped and feared, the blow, when it does come, is indeed grievous; but it cannot be compared to the unspeakable anguish and regret which are felt when they are snatched from us suddenly. We always cling to the thought that if we could only have had a few moments with them before the lips and eyes were closed and silent for ever, we could have borne our sorrow better.

Who can say what Kate felt as she bent over him, deaf to all entreaties not to stay any longer?

" Oh, papa, papa! what are you thinking of now?" she exclaimed. "I would give worlds to know, poor dead darling! Did you think of me away from you in gaiety and health, father love, in your last short agony? Are you quite sure, Aunt Neta, he did not mention me?"

"Come away, Kate! come away, I beseech you!" said her husband, as he took her hand, and tried to get her out of the room; "it will do you harm staying here so long. Do come."

"Good-bye, papa," she said, half-turning to go away. "I should never have left you, then this would have been spared me. Every one gone now—mother, baby, father—every one I loved dearly." Her long-denied tears came, as she gave the last kiss to the dead lips; and Lord Denton led her away, and laid her on her sofa, feeling that her last remark was verily and indeed true. As he sat by her side and coaxed her to take some refreshment, the unasked confession kept ringing in his ears, and he wondered *what* he could do to make his wife love him. He had certainly tried to be

all that he ought to be to her, and yet there
was the fact,—she had herself said before him
and her aunt that "all" she had loved on
earth were gone.

It was no use saying anything to her now
in her great grief,—he must hope she did not
really mean what she had said.

All Mr. Byrne's affairs were in perfect
order, his will and papers arranged, so that
there was very little trouble in settling
everything. His income was almost equally
divided between his daughter and sister-in-
law. A diamond ring, which he had always
worn, he had bequeathed to his young friend
Bartle Blake, a few legacies to friends and
servants, and some to two or three of the
Dublin charities. They agreed to keep the
house as a place to come to for change, so
for the present it was shut up, and left in
charge of a couple of old faithful domestics,
Miss Casteldi willingly accepting Lord Denton's offer of making their house her home.

So they all went back to Denton Court, where
they stayed the rest of that year, seeing no
company beyond their immediate neighbours
and the county families who came to offer
their condolences. Helen Leigh was often
with her. Kate's grief soon became less
keen, and she found herself longing for
change and excitement almost before the
new year had fairly set in, with frost and
snow and every appearance of some severe
winter weather.

CHAPTER III.

NE day, when Kate and her aunt were sitting alone, Miss Casteldi looked up, and found her niece holding her face in her hand, as if she was in pain. They had said very little to each other since breakfast, when Kate had been surprised and annoyed at finding no letter from her husband in the post-bag. He had been away for some days on business matters, and, as a rule, she always had had a letter every day from him; but on this morning she was disappointed, and told her aunt how vexed she felt.

"Perhaps he is coming home to-day, and therefore thought it was useless to write," said Miss Casteldi.

"Useless, aunt!" exclaimed Kate. "How absurd of you to say such a thing. If he is coming, the more reason for writing."

"Well, my dear Kate, I am sorry I have angered you; I did not mean to do so. He may be ill, or by some unforeseen circumstance been too late for this morning's post, and you will get one, perhaps, this evening."

"It really matters very little indeed, Aunt Neta, whether I do or not. It has grown quite a habit with me to look for a daily letter when he is away from home, but after all I need scarcely regret the not getting one, as there is very little variety in any of my husband's letters," said Kate, getting up hastily from the table, and leaving the room.

Her kind aunt had seen so much of Kate's wilfulness since she had lived in their house, that she could not help feeling, in spite of all her love for Kate, that she was very much to blame for so utterly disregarding her husband's happiness. She saw that he lived

one life and her niece another. There was
no confidence, no unison between them:
they were cold and distant; and if at any
time Lord Denton made some approach to
fondness and attention, Kate gave as little
response to it as she would have given to a
slave. There was certainly no open breach
between them, and perhaps a less loving,
anxious eye than Miss Casteldi's would not
have noticed so much the want of the thousand
and one nameless little indications of a happy
married life; but she felt that almost every
day the difference was growing greater, and
that Kate was more faulty than she could
have believed had she not had distinct proof
before her very eyes of her shortcomings.
So she determined, the first favourable opportunity, to remonstrate with Kate, and point
out to her where she failed in her wifely
duty. She usually sat with her in her morn-
ing-room, where they generally sewed or
wrote letters, or arranged about dress, visits,

&c., and had their little confidences entirely
to themselves. When Miss Casteldi joined
Kate on the morning mentioned in the com-
mencement of this chapter, she began her
carpet-work, hoping her niece would perhaps
make some mention of the subject they had
talked of at breakfast. Kate, however, did
not speak, but a heavy sigh from her caused
her aunt to go to her side, and place her arm
round her, saying,—

" What is it, Kate, love ? Are you ill ?"

A small piece of delicate lace and muslin
lay on Kate's lap, and Miss Casteldi saw that
it had caused this emotion. It was a part of
some baby-work which had lain hidden in
the work-basket all these long months, and
which Kate had accidentally taken up again.
Kate did not reply at once,—her heart seemed
too full for words.

" No, Aunt Neta, I am not ill, thank you;
not in body at least, but I am very, very
weary to-day. I have been thinking how

utterly desolate and solitary I should be if anything happened to you."

"I wonder at your saying such things, Kate, indeed I do," replied her aunt, sorrowfully. "You cannot mean what you say— you forget your husband."

"Indeed, I do not," replied Kate. "It is because I do think of him that I say this to you."

"Oh, Kate, my precious girl! unsay those words. You are gloomy, and unlike yourself this morning."

"Would you have me deceive you, Aunt Neta?" said Kate, slowly and solemnly; "because, if not, I cannot unsay them. I would that I were side by side with my little child or my darling father. I shall never be happy again. This is the cloud I dreamed of, and I shall never see through it."

"But why, Kate? What reason have you to say this? What makes you so discontented? Your husband is devoted to you,

or would be if you did not drift so far away
from him with your icy coldness; and you
have every wish and whim gratified with
every luxury and indulgence."

" I dare say you are right, aunt. I should
perhaps be far happier without all these
things. I cannot tell; but this I know, that
I never have had, and never shall have, any
confidence in Lord Denton. I cannot say
why, or give any reason for feeling such
utter want of faith in him. He never leaves
me but what my mind is for ever asking
itself all sorts of questions as to what he
does, and where he goes. I never know
what he is doing. He does not tell me the
truth about his movements ; and that he goes
to places and does things which he keeps
from my knowledge I feel certain of. What
they are I neither know nor care."

" But Kate, dear, are you sure of it, or is
it only what you fancy?" asked her aunt.
"You can scarcely be surprised at your

husband seeking pleasure and amusements away from a home that is made so cheerless to him."

"I don't know what you mean, aunt. What do you expect me to do? Does Lord Denton want me to run after and amuse him like a small child? I always thought him old enough to manage without so much looking after."

"You purposely misunderstand me, Kate. You know what I mean. You know you are not kind and loving and attentive as a wife ought to be; and you know that your husband just pines for a kind word, and some show of affection from you, which he never gets, and which, since you married him, I think he has a right to expect from you."

"I made a mistake, Aunt Neta, when I married, as I dare say many others have done before me. I thought that wealth and position would be all I should care for; with them I thought life would be perfect. I found I had deceived myself before I returned from my wedding trip. I cannot respect my husband, who has no will of his own, and is as easily led to good or ill as a senseless boy."

" Oh, my dear Kate, this is indeed grievous to me. I am pained beyond words to describe. But do tell me more; tell me the real cause of all this. Why do you come to such conclusions about him? He seems to me so good and kind-hearted."

" I quite agree with you, aunt. He is, as you say, all goodness and attention; but even if he does love me as he has so often said, I feel certain that there is something— But there, I need say no more, Aunt Neta; let this never pass your lips to living mortal, I entreat you. I had better, perhaps, have kept silent even to you. I am so sorry to have distressed you" (seeing tears falling down her aunt's cheeks); " but I was vexed with showing so much temper to you this morning, and indeed at various other times, that I thought

if I made a kind of confession to you as to
how things were going on, you would see
how much I have to make me irritable and
cross, and make allowances for me. But
don't cry, dear Aunt Neta, I am not unhappy always; on the contrary, I have had
a great deal of pleasure and much enjoyment since I married. It is only now and
then, when I get gloomy, and think about the
past, and what might have been, that I give
way to all this, which after all is, perhaps,
more fancy than reality. Had baby lived,
everything would have been so different. It
would have been a bond between us that I
fear now will never be; and it does seem
hard that the one thing we both most long
for should be denied us."

Poor Miss Casteldi made no reply to this.
She was thinking of how little good she had
done by talking to her niece. She had said
so little of what she had resolved to say
when opportunity offered, and saw that it

was almost hopeless to remonstrate : for Kate
evidently fancied herself wronged in some
way which she appeared not to care to tell
her the particulars of, and of course it was
impossible for her to know if she had or had
not any just grounds for her suspicions and
doubts of her husband's truth. She was more
perplexed than ever, and began to think
that perhaps she too had made a mistake in
coming to live in her niece's home. Especially
as she felt it so impossible to mend matters
in the least, her wisest course was to say no
more either one way or the other, and wait
and hope.

The evening's bag brought the truant
letter, which was dated from a Rectory in
one of the Midland Counties, and Lord Denton
told Kate that he was just paying a pop-visit
to an old fellow who used to coach him in
younger days, and that he hoped to return
to the Court on the following evening. So,
very soon after the announcement came, the

writer followed, looking bored and tired, and
complaining of fatigue, which was a very unusual thing for him; and, before we take
leave of him for the present, we will see how
he has occupied the last day or two, and
what took him to the Rectory he wrote from.

A letter which he found at his Club had
made him resolve to stay a day or two longer
in town; but while he was reading his morning
paper, a telegram came to him, which considerably altered his plans, and caused him
to consult a Bradshaw, take a Hansom, and
drive rapidly to The Albany, make a hasty
call upon his friend Captain Martin, with
whom he swallowed a bumper of brandy and
soda-water, and then they went off together
to the Euston Station. The Captain did not
accompany his friend on the journey. Whatever the business was that was taking Lord
Denton away so suddenly, he evidently
knew all about it, and had come so far with
him to talk it over. They both stood till

the last moment at the carriage-door. When
his friend got in, Martin said, giving him a
parting slap on the shoulder,—

"Good-bye, old fellow; if anything hap-
pens I'll see it's all right, and run down
when you let me know."

The train moved on, and Captain Martin
went leisurely back to the West End.

A white-haired, comfortable looking clerical
gentleman met Lord Denton at the end of
his journey. They were evidently friends,
as the greeting they gave each other was
very cordial.

"How is he now, Gresham?" said his
Lordship, eagerly. "Not worse, I hope?"

"No, not worse, thank God! I feared he
would be gone before you could get here;
but he has rallied a little, and Simpson seems
to be a trifle more sanguine about him. He
is still with him, and I have asked him
to-day to see you, of course not mentioning
names."

"Oh, thank you, I would just as soon hear his account from you; but as he is waiting, I suppose I must see him," replied Lord Denton, looking sadly worried.

"I thought it better to send for you," said Mr. Gresham, "and waited till I feared to wait longer. We lost one of our boys last week before his friends got here, which has made me a little nervous and fidgety, I dare say."

"Oh, certainly, certainly; you are quite right. I would rather you at any time do so if there is the slightest necessity. Poor lad! God knows I do not wish to neglect him. Will he know me, do you think?"

"Not just now; I am certain he will not. He was quite delirious this morning, and did not even recognize my wife or myself."

The doctor was more confident about the little sufferer. When he saw Lord Denton, he said, "that in all probability, if the sleep which had come on the last half-hour lasted any time, he would wake up better. He would look in again in a few hours, and hoped the most perfect quiet would be kept about the sick-room." So Lord Denton had to wait, harassed and impatient as he was, and while waiting, penned his letter to his wife, which was too late for that evening's post.

It was far on into the early next morning before he was admitted to the boy's room, where on tiptoe he went to the bed-side and leaned over him. A faint smile lighted up for an instant the invalid's face, which Lord Denton took for recognition. It was probably nothing of the kind; however, he was glad to find that the medical man the following morning considered him out of present danger; and as he could be of little or no use there, and wanted to return to Denton, he left after a hasty luncheon and taking another peep into the sick-room.

As far as the child's interest and welfare

were concerned, he could not have been
anywhere where he would have been better
tended or carefully watched. Mrs. Gresham
was a gentlewoman, refined and motherly.
She had no family of her own, and was
really very fond of children, so that her husband's taking six pupils was not a task to
her. On the contrary, she took great pleasure
in winning their confidences, and was a
favourite with all of them. They had a
pretty house and grounds, plenty of fine
country around them, and although Mr.
Gresham worked them pretty hard, they had
altogether a happy home there. A fever
broke out in the village near, and in spite of
every care taken to prevent it spreading to
them, they were dismayed one morning to
find one of the boys complaining of sickness
and sore throat. There was no mistaking,
the enemy had come. They sent the five
other boys away with the tutor a few miles.
The first victim died; but although they had

sent the others away, in a few short days
another, the youngest, was stricken down, and
remained for nearly a week between life and
death. He, however, ultimately recovered,
and as soon as he was able to move and travel
he was taken south by good Mrs. Gresham,
who was herself thoroughly worn out with
anxiety and watching, and needing a change
almost as badly as her little charge. He was
a gentle, loving child, of about seven years
of age, had a nice open countenance, and a
good deal of animation about him; passionately fond of his friend and almost mother, in
whose house he had been nearly five years.
He used to call her mamma, and sometimes
say at the same time, "You are not my real
mamma, you know, for my mamma is dead
and buried, and gone to Heaven; but I love
you quite as much almost." He was a very
much younger charge than Mrs. Gresham
had ever undertaken. A tiny, talking
creature, of a little over two, was a very

different undertaking to what she had been accustomed to,—boys of from ten to sixteen or eighteen. But her husband had been under great obligations to Lord Denton; and when he wrote asking them to take the child, as he was anxious to find a home for him immediately where he could place him in safety and confidence, his mother having just died, they took him cheerfully and willingly, and had never once regretted doing so. What made Lord Denton interested in him they did not know. Whose son he was, or what his birth was, they did not ask ; and until he had been with them some time, and had become very dear to both of them, they did not know anything definite about him.

Lord Denton came to see him occasionally, took him out, and gave him anything he wished for; and Captain Martin generally came to see him when Lord Denton was abroad or unable to go there from any other cause. Daily accounts of his convalescence were sent to Lord Denton, and after a few weeks of the sea-side, where he regained the use of his legs, and got back some colour in his cheeks, he returned to the old country-house, where we must leave him for the present.

It will be seen by this account of him that Lady Denton did not know of his existence. Whatever motives Lord Denton had for secrecy were shared only by his friend and companion, Captain Martin. Whether he was wise in excluding his wife from his confidence, or whether she would have made a better *confidante* than the Captain, we will wait till we know more of the child's history to determine.

CHAPTER IV.

IT is now perhaps time to mention how Mr. Blake managed to get on in Russia, where he was going when we last heard of him. He found that his appointment would necessitate close study and application, which, considering the state of his mind at the time, was the very best thing for him. There is nothing like hard work, either of the head or hands, to help us over heart-wounds, especially if we set to work with the determination to forget them. He did not make friends as quickly as he might have done, for he had letters of introduction to some very good families. He interested himself in the manners and customs of the

country, and gave much of his spare time
to making notes for future use. His employers
soon found, to their satisfaction and benefit,
that they had hit upon a most trustworthy
and clever man, under whose direction their
work was progressing very favourably. But
after a year or so, people began to find out,
somehow, that he could sing and play well.
Then the fair relatives of the few gentlemen he knew often invited him to drop in
during the very long or the very short evenings, as the case might be, in the easy Con-
tinental fashion, for tea and talk and music.

He had heard of Kate's engagement, and
then saw her marriage announced in a London
paper. His jealous fancy had thought of this
immediately after that never-to-be-forgotten
conversation in the library at The Ridgway.
Still he had given her credit for purer and
better motives than those she herself owned
to having; and although he had been unfortunate enough to woo and not win her,

he sincerely hoped that her choice had
fallen on one who would be all she desired
and deserved. Of course he could not help
wondering about her sometimes, but he purposely refrained from asking any questions
about her when writing to mutual friends,
as he could not have allowed them to come to
her ears. Once married she was so far out of
his reach, sacredly, so purely another's, that
his strict sense of honour would not permit
him to indulge himself in even thinking of
her but as a treasure lost to him for ever;
and until he had thoroughly crushed out all
his former feeling for her, he resolved, if
possible, not to come to England, where he
would run the risk of meeting her. All
honour to him for his bravery. If the same
kind of right feeling was more generally
held to be correct and proper among men
of the present day, perhaps there would be
fewer wretched homes, husbands, wives, and
children, less misery and crime, which de-

moralizes our present social life, and is a
blot upon and a disgrace to our prosperous,
beautiful country.

He heard from Mr. Byrne's lawyer, and
received the ring safely which had been left
for him, and which he had so often seen on
his friend's finger. At first he thought he
would write to Lady Denton, and express
the sympathy he so truly felt at her loss; but
upon reflection he resolved not to do it, and
contented himself with writing to the man of
business, acknowledging his having received
the ring. He had by this time become on
very friendly terms with a family of the
name of Nitikin. The father and two sons
held government appointments; there were
three young daughters, the second one, named
Olga, was particularly fond of singing, and
played extremely well, and was always glad
when they added to the number of their
musical friends. They all spoke English,
and were lively, pleasant girls, very socially

disposed, rather nice-looking, with the blood-
and-milk complexion which in Russia is considered the perfection of beauty. As their
father was a wealthy man, in a very good
position, there was some of the best society
to be met at their house. Bartle found a
good deal of enjoyment awaiting him there
whenever he cared to leave his bachelor's
quarters and refresh himself with the variety
and amusement offered him, with so much
genuine good-will. He got to feel quite at
home there, and made himself very agreeable
and useful to them. He sometimes sang
to oblige his fair friends at the amateur con-
certs which so often take place in Russia
(given by the ladies for charitable purposes;
they sell the tickets at a high figure, and
sometimes make large profits); and they made
so much of him, and praised his voice so
highly, that a less sensible person would have
become terribly conceited. Of course this
kind of thing brought him a good deal in

contact with Olga Nitikin. He fancied he
saw some likeness to Kate in her, but that
was simply imagination, as no two people
could possibly be more unlike each other:
her voice may have resembled Kate's a little,
but nothing more. And so time passed on
pleasantly, and his friends heard of his prosperity, and wondered when he would come
to pay a visit to them, and whether he would
marry and settle there for good. He had
written only very rarely to Mrs. Leigh. She
would fain have known more about him; but
beyond gathering from what he said that he
was satisfied and happy, and would be sure
to come to see her whenever he came to
England, she knew nothing; and she and
Helen often talked about him, and what he
would be likely to do.

"I hope he will marry soon," said Mrs.
Leigh. "Young men are far better off, even
though they may have to work a little harder
and get less spare time to throw away upon

trifles, with a wife and a home to interest themselves in."

"Well, mamma, my opinion is that he will never marry any one now. He is just the kind of man to whom a disappointment such as he had would be so bitter, that he never will make the attempt to risk the chance of another. Besides I know he loved Kate so dearly that he won't be likely to love again," said Helen, turning very red, and looking intently out of the window, to prevent her mother noticing her.

"Time heals all wounds, Nellie," replied her mother. "I dare say he has forgotten the old love already."

"Well then, mamma, I do hope he will come and take a wife from his own country. I never liked the idea of mixed marriages you know, and I certainly should like him to marry some one very nice indeed."

"I expect, Nellie," said her mother, smiling, "he need not come home to do that; for I believe the Russian ladies are very clever and very charming."

" Perhaps they are, mamma; but I said ' nice,' and I mean it, which is not either charming or clever; in fact, I can't very well explain the meaning I have for that pet word of mine."

Mrs. Leigh was about this time surprised by a visit from their friend Mr. Benson. Business matters had not brought him over to The Ridgway now, at least not the same kind of business as the last. During Helen's short stay with them at Broughton, before she joined the Dentons for the Scotch tour, Mr. Benson, junior, had taken the opportunity of telling her that he hoped to have the felicity of making her, some future day, Mrs. Benson. This young gentleman was by no means as *brusque* and disagreeable as his father; he had pleasant manners, and was generally liked by young ladies. His father frequently called him " a lazy dog," and

often added "he was not worth his salt";
but these facts did not appear to distress his
son and heir, or make him work better or
improve him in any way. He had a decided
liking and turn for all the lighter and vainer
indulgences of this wicked world, much to
his respected father's disgust and displeasure.
The old man could not understand how *his*
only son could have a dislike for work.

"He must have inherited it from his
mother's side, I'm certain, for no Benson
ever yet was lazy," he used to say. The
father had educated him for his own pro-
fession, in the hope that when he became
old himself, and not able to do so much, the
younger hands would take off some of the
work, and be of service to him. He was,
however, sadly disappointed, for the lad did
not like law; he wanted to go into the
army, which made his father more determined than ever to keep him at the desk,
and make him work with him. So, when

the youth found his father would not give
in, he gave up the idea of wearing a red
coat, and perhaps did his best at home,
though the best was bad enough. He had no
energy or application, was not reliable, and
always behindhand. He, as he grew older,
would occasionally suggest to Mr. Benson that
he ought to take a partner,—" Some one you
know, sir, who is pretty well up to hard
work."—" To indulge you in your confounded laziness, I suppose, you mean," his
father would reply, feeling at the same time
the necessity of taking his son's advice.

Some time after Helen had left them, young
Benson told his father that he had made
her an offer, and that she had decidedly
refused him. This was very annoying to
the old man, as he had had a pet scheme
for some years, and that was the marrying
his boy to Helen Leigh. He had watched
and noticed her for that reason only. He
knew she was good and industrious, and

in every way fitted to rule a house and husband, he thought, with care and decision, —just the girl to be an ornament to a house, and not one who would for ever be wanting to gad about here and there; and he had fancied that the young folks had got on very well together; and he wondered why Miss Helen had refused him. He would go and talk it over with her mother; it was all nonsense: she only wanted to be asked again,—it was quite time she married; and he resolved to get away for a few days as soon as he could, and see what the mother said about it. He had a great idea about parents "making" their children do as they were bid, and he never for a moment doubted that Mrs. Leigh would wish her daughter to make the match offered to her; therefore, he had only to put it to her in a sensible manner, and she would, he hoped, see it in the same light as he did.

Mr. Benson entirely forgot how unsuccess-

ful he had been with his own son, and how
little he had been able to "make" him do.
As a rule, we find those parents whose
children are not the best specimens of good
training, too ready to advise and conjure
other parents to allow only this or that, to
be sure not to do so-and-so; and when
they find that their advice is not taken
(fortunately), they predict a sorry future for
their friends' children, and forget to look
at home. When Mr. Benson had mentioned
to Mrs. Leigh, a few years before, that possibly Helen and his son might come together, she made no objection, except that
they were both too young for anything of
the kind to be thought of just then. She
really rather liked the young man, but of
course said they must see more of each
other, and that Helen must be left entirely
to make her own choice. This was quite
enough encouragement for Mr. Benson; he
looked upon the thing as settled, taking care

to tell the young hopeful what good fortune was in store for him if he behaved himself, and was contented to wait, inviting Helen pretty often to his house. It never once occurred to him that she might have other views or any scruples. So after patiently waiting, and everything going on as he thought satisfactorily, he was surprised to find the lady had dared to say No! And if his son could be relied on for truth in the matter, she had said it most positively. So after a good deal of deliberation on the subject, he thought he would, for his own peace of mind, go and see the coy damsel, and, if necessary, give her a scolding for her " nonsense," as he called it.

Helen had, of course, told her mother when she returned home of Mr. Benson's offer, and Mrs. Leigh saw in a moment that it was most distasteful to her daughter, and she resolved never to have it mentioned between them again. So she was not at all surprised to see the father; in fact, she had wondered why he had not written to her upon the subject, and knew that that, and that only, had brought him to The Ridgway. Poor Mr. Benson, he was doomed to be very disappointed! He found Mrs. Leigh sorry for him and his son too, but perfectly sure that Helen had done wisely in refusing to allow any hope, as she never had had, and never could have, any feeling but friendship for the young man; therefore it was worse than useless to endeavour to prolong the idea of anything of the kind ever happening between them.

There was no mistaking or disputing Mrs. Leigh's calm, decisive manner, so Mr. Benson went away more ill tempered than ever, he not having had the chance of saying a cutting sentence to the object of his severe displeasure. Mrs. Leigh, before he left, after their confidential interview, positively forbade any allusion to be made to the affair before Helen. She was nervous and not in very good health, and no good results could come of unnecessary bickerings.

As he was rattled on to the busy town where he lived, Mr. Benson grumbled at women (especially young ones) to his heart's content. Helen fell a great many degrees in his estimation during that journey. "She wasn't a bit better than the rest of them," he mentally exclaimed, as he betook himself again to his beloved papers; and his son knew very well that his father had been to the Leighs, although he had not breathed a word about having been there to him.

It may as well be here mentioned that not very long after this Mr. Benson junior soothed his rejected feelings, and took to himself a wife from the town in which he lived, who had a large fortune, and loved him very dearly. She had a very grand wedding, to which both Helen and her mother were invited, and no one more heartily wished the happy pair every future blessing that this world can give than did the bridegroom's first love and her mother. Old Mr. Benson was in great spirits. He began to think that, perhaps, after all, nothing could have been better than the present state of things, and when his first little grandchild was born, he thawed out of his cold, disagreeable manner wonderfully. Every one remarked upon the improvement in him, which was almost entirely due to the influence of tiny hands and loving words from a wee image of himself, as people told him.

The marriage turned out an exceedingly fortunate one; and as no one but our old friend Mr. Benson is likely to be mentioned in this story again, we will bid them adieu, and return to Lady Denton.

CHAPTER V.

HERE was little if any change in Kate's life for the next few years. In spite of her earnest desire for children, she did not again become a mother. They spent their time between the seasons either on the Continent or somewhere away from Denton Court. The house was almost as much deserted as before Lord Denton married. This was much regretted by all their acquaintances, who saw so little of them during the few short visits they made there. The house, which had given so much satisfaction to Kate when she was taken there a bride, had become distasteful to her, and, for reasons

which she never explained, she avoided as
much as possible staying there at all. Lady
Denton's love of excitement and pleasure
had by no means diminished; on the contrary, she tried to live on in an unceasing
round of gaiety. She was very much sought
after everywhere she went, and found plenty
of admirers and flatterers to do homage to
her beauty and charming voice. Every year
she seemed, instead of tiring of so much
frivolity, with its constant wear and tear, to
enter into it with fresh zest and animation,
and became one of the most fashionable
leaders of the gay world in and out of
London.

As to Lord Denton, he was very seldom
in attendance upon his stately wife. His
love and attention had so often been repulsed,
that one can scarcely wonder at his finding
more congenial companionship. He made
a desperate effort to be something akin to
what he ought to have been when he married

Kate, and had she only then given him a helping hand, in all probability she might have altered him wonderfully. But, alas! she found out very soon his weak points, and despised him for them, till she took no pains to hide her indifference from him. They never quarrelled, or in any way clashed with each other, and very few of their friends even supposed they were not an averagely happy couple, so perfectly polite and proper was their manner in society when they were to be seen together.

Miss Casteldi accompanied Kate about everywhere as much as she found her health was equal to; and often, when she would have been very glad to have stayed quietly at home, she unselfishly resolved to make an effort and go with her, as she felt it was the only good she could do to Kate to watch over her and protect her as much as possible.

Lord Denton saw his friend Captain Martin very frequently. They had almost returned to the old life again, and the former left no stone unturned, as it were, to keep his friend away from his wife and home. Lady Denton and he had not become any better friends: her haughty coldness to him was so pointed, so perceptible to every one, that he came in for a far larger amount of bantering about it than he was able to swallow with comfort. Of course they often met, here, there, and everywhere; she not caring to avoid him out of her own house, he not losing a single opportunity of throwing himself in her way. But the sudden change which came over her manner whenever he came near to where she was, told plainly enough how much she disliked his being near her. All this was gall and wormwood to Captain Martin, and he hated her so much, that, as he could not in any way make her suffer for her contempt, he redoubled his efforts to strengthen his influence over her husband and lead him into excesses

the knowledge of which must come sooner
or later to the wife's ears. He found little
difficulty in carrying out his designs upon
his pliable and good-natured friend, who fell
readily enough into all the temptations held
out to him. Captain Martin's real motives
were, perhaps, hardly allowed even to himself, bad man as he was. He hoped and
believed that, by leaving Kate so much
alone, surrounded as she was in her glorious
beauty and youth by so many admirers, she
would not be proof against the many snares
around her, and that one day she would sink
to the level he desired. Not that Lord
Denton ever breathed to him, intimate as
they were, a word about his wife's indifference; but, man of the world as he was,
he knew perfectly well that there was no
real love between them. He saw that pretty
plainly the first season he spent in London
after they met at Nice, and everything
which had happened since then only made

assurance doubly sure. But certainly for
once in his wicked life Captain Martin had
made a mistake. He little knew the woman
whose destruction he hoped for. Whatever
Kate's faults and weaknesses were, they
were not such as would lead her to any
actual violation of the duties she had taken
upon herself. Her marriage was, perhaps, a
sin in the first place, but having made that
mistake, she would never try to repair or
alter it by taking a step which would bring
disgrace upon her own fair fame and her
husband's honour. No slight or reflection
of any kind could be cast upon her even by
the most malicious scandal-lover of society.
Vain and frivolous she was, but pure in
thought, word, and deed.

Among the many friends Lady Denton
made in London was an Hon. Mrs. Gilbert,
whom she met at a crowded reception, and
who made a good deal of fuss about the
pleasure she felt in meeting her, as she

had known Mr. Byrne and his young wife,
—"before you were born, my dear," she
added, smiling. This was quite enough to
make Kate perfectly ready to chat with her,
and accept her offer of calling upon her
the next day. They were, after that, very
constantly seen together, and Mrs. Gilbert
managed to make a good deal of use of
Lady Denton's fashionable carriages.

It would have been difficult to guess cor-
rectly how many years had gone by since Mrs.
Gilbert first knew Mr. Byrne. She dressed
so youthfully, was so quick, and had such
an abundant flow of spirits and conversation,
that she might have been taken for any age
between thirty-five and forty-five or fifty,
without any great mistake as to outward
and visible signs. She had good teeth
and plenty of fine hair, few wrinkles and
bright eyes; so that time had indeed passed
lightly over her, as she was really within
one year of the last-mentioned figure. She

married, when about twenty-nine, a young
lieutenant, some years younger than she
was—ran away with him from Ireland.

They were both very poor, so they lived
abroad, to economize their slender means.
He was thin and frightened, she bold and
daring to a degree seldom, fortunately, met
with in a woman; and after a few years
of not very enviable conjugal bliss, he died,
and all their friends then began to pity him,
abuse her, and declare that she had simply
worried his poor existence out of him. Be
that as it may, she did very, very soon put
off all appearance of grief, and became a
constant frequenter of the various notorious
gaming-tables. Her friends were all rather
taken by surprise, when, years after, she made
her appearance in London, took a neat mode-
rate-sized house near Belgrave Square, and
set up a comfortable establishment. There
was no end of different reports and conjec-
tures as to how she had gained the means to

do so. No one had died to leave her any property—that every one knew, or thought they knew; both her own and her husband's connexions were as poor as church mice, and had too many to come in for a share, if there had been anything to leave, for her to have had any considerable sum. Of course Mrs. Gilbert knew every one was most anxious to ascertain all about her and her belongings; but she did not care a button-top for any one, and took particular precautions for their not being able to find out. She appeared to have everything that was necessary for a refined, luxurious life, gave pleasant little dinner and supper parties, received some of the best society, and was to be met everywhere. The commotion and wonderment caused by her unexpected appearance soon subsided; other, and perhaps more exciting matters, came to set that aside, and Mrs. Gilbert enjoyed her gains in peace and quiet.

Play had either soured her temper or else she had never possessed a good one. No woman living could possibly have said harder or more spiteful things about people than she did. She was a dear lover of scandal, and never scrupled to repeat to any one, whether they wished to hear or not, any bit of slander she could get hold of, with her own highly-coloured additions. She had a great dislike to growing old, just because she had none of the pleasant quieter resources of old age to fall back upon, and was always doubly severe on those who were young and beautiful, especially if they showed that they did not particularly care for her society. She had an exceedingly retentive memory—some one said of it once that it was like a living dictionary, with the faults and failings of all her friends ranged in alphabetical order.

She had frequently met Lord Denton before his marriage at some of the before-mentioned

tables with old friends, and knew more
about his former life than most people did.
She heard of his marriage, and knew to
a shade what fortune his wife had, and all
about her temper, coldness, &c. This had
been supplied to her by Captain Martin.

There was no difficulty in such a woman
finding out Kate's weak points; her busy
tongue was far less bitter when talking to
her than to any one else. She knew so many
families at Kate's house, or pretended she
knew, had travelled and seen so much of
life, that she made herself quite an agreeable
companion, and won Kate's confidence
easily. Miss Casteldi did not take as great
a fancy to her as Kate did; still, she went
to her supper-parties sometimes, and stayed
for a quiet rubber afterwards. Not that
quiet rubbers were the order of the day (or
rather night) at Mrs. Gilbert's—only those
visitors not on very intimate terms with her
were invited to join in that game : a select

few met pretty often for far more exciting
and risky amusement. Mrs. Gilbert "loved"
cards and dice with a grasping, unsatiable
devotion. She never tired of them, and sat
far into the night, with unflagging patience,
either winning or losing, with perfect cool-
ness. It did not take Mrs. Gilbert long to
find out Lady Denton's leaning towards
cards, and she had no difficulty in leading
her on from the "quiet rubber" to the more
fascinating gambling chance-work, when, of
course, Kate had to go there without the
attendance of her aunt.

Mrs. Gilbert knew well enough that Miss
Casteldi would have taken fright at the bare
idea of such goings on, and took care that
she was kept in ignorance of the coils which
were fast folding themselves around her un-
suspecting niece. Kate lost large sums of
money,—at times she did occasionally win;
but upon the whole, if she had not had such
an extravagant carelessness about money, she

would have been appalled at the amount.
But she had a handsome income of her own,
for which to no one had she any need to
be accountable, therefore whatever gave her
most pleasure she did not scruple to use it
for. Mrs. Gilbert managed everything very
cleverly and quietly. When Lady Denton
was at her house alone in the evening, she
had given express orders that neither Captain
Martin, Lord Denton, nor a few others of
their set should be admitted. A man-servant
whom she had brought from the Continent
with her, and who was in her confidence,
understood all the ins and outs of the arrangements, and generally carried out her wishes
very cleverly. Etienne was " a perfect treasure," Mrs. Gilbert often said, and " she
wouldn't part with him for worlds."

One morning, as Lady Denton was going
down to a late breakfast, she met her husband
on the stairs, and he, with a touch of his old
fondness, placed his arm on her waist, and

turned to accompany her downstairs. Kate
was feeling rather more genial than she
usually did to him, and they entered the
breakfast-room together.

"I am going to the Countess of C——'s
garden-party this afternoon," Kate said, "and
I want you to go with me."

"Oh, certainly, with great pleasure," replied Lord Denton. "I am off just now to
look in at Tattersall's, but I have nothing to
do there to keep me any time, so I will be
sure to be back again to luncheon."

Nothing more was said about it, and, after
discussing some other engagements, he went
out, and Kate prepared for her morning ride.
At luncheon no Lord Denton appeared. Kate
ate her own in silence, and immediately after
went to her aunt's room, where she stayed
till it was time to go to dress. Miss Casteldi
had a nervous headache, and was quite unable
to lift her head off her pillow. She had been
subject to such ailments more or less all her

life, and although she had had the best medical
advice, she found nothing did her so much
good as perfect quiet and rest. Kate was
very kind and attentive to her during these
attacks, and, when she could do nothing
better, she would sit by her bed-side, and be
ready to give her drink or turn her hot pillow.

Norah put the finishing touches to her
mistress's charming toilette, which became
Kate wonderfully well. One of Kate's good
qualities was punctuality; she was seldom or
ever later than she intended to be. For one
thing, she had not learned to fritter hours
and hours away at her glass, as so many
fashionable women do; she always decided
what she would wear easily, and as easily
put it on. As yet, her beauty did not require
the numberless touches here and there that
advancing years and rounds of constant dissipation make necessary to hide their ravages
from the vulgar gaze. When Kate was quite
ready, she rang to know if his Lordship

was at home; his valet replied in the nega-
tive.

"I might have known," she exclaimed to
herself angrily, as she drew on her delicate
tinted gloves, far too hastily for their chance
of keeping whole. "Fool that I was to ask
or expect it!"

She stood, before she left her room, de-
bating whether she should give him a few
minutes' grace: took out her tiny watch, and
found it was already past the time she intended to start. She went hastily down
stairs, told the coachman to drive quickly,
and never looked to the right or left, fearing
even to catch a glimpse of her husband, if
by chance he was hurrying home in the hope
of being in time.

Oh, how angry she was as she drove
along! how bitterly she reproached him
again and again! Why was he not there?
If she could not rely upon his keeping a
promise made only a few hours before, what

could she do? He would come later on, she
felt certain, full of contrite apologies, to one
of which she would not listen. She would accept no excuse for this rudeness. For reasons
best known to herself, she had particularly
wished to appear with him to-day, and had
told him so, and he *ought* to come at any
cost. As she whirled along in her luxurious
carriage, she could not help aggravating her
already ruffled temper by picturing to herself
how things had changed with her,—how the
man who had made such a show of affection,
such vows of love and devotion, could now
leave her almost as much alone as if they
were nothing to each other. She almost felt
to hate him at that moment, and went over
in her mind all sorts of disagreeable scenes,
in which she resolved to show him how
thoroughly she despised him and his deceit,
and that she could live and enjoy life without
any of his attentions. Then she thought of
her dead baby, whom she had never seen,

and wished it had lived to love her, and give her something to do and to love; and thinking of it softened her and brought tears to her eyes, which, if she could have allowed them to come freely, would have relieved her full, aching heart. But this was no time or place for tears, so, gulping down as best she could "her lump in the throat," she immediately after was set down at the pretty residence of the Countess.

CHAPTER VI.

LADY DENTON was among the first guests who arrived at the retreat of their distinguished hostess. Small additions to the party began soon to follow her rapidly, and before long a brilliant, gay throng of elegantly-dressed men and women filled the house and grounds. Kate was soon surrounded by friends and admirers, chatting and smiling with her usual natural ease and grace. Would any one have dreamed, to see her thus, that she was really very miserable at heart? Of course there were many inquiries about her husband. She replied, "That perhaps he would come later on; some engagement which he had in the morning was keeping him, she feared; he would perhaps come to fetch her away." This was quite true; she did, indeed, feel almost certain of seeing him there, and kept looking and watching the arrivals till she knew it was useless to do so any longer. As she was returning to her carriage, she heard her friend Mrs. Gilbert say to some ladies who were leaving, "Oh! thank you, no. If you will excuse me, I will beg a seat of Lady Denton; she is going home alone, I know, and passes my door, so good-bye." As she took her seat beside Kate, she said, "That as she knew she had no one with her, she thought she would offer her company and give up the seat she had had coming down, which was not, to say the best of it, the most comfortable she had ever sat in." She added, smiling, "One of four is a great squeeze, I assure you." Kate smiled too, but heartily wished her friend, for once, far away.

How the word "alone" had been repeated to her that afternoon! Every one
seemed to notice it to her, as if it was an
unprecedented occurrence for her to be seen
anywhere without her husband. People
might have known that she had been disappointed and annoyed at his not being
there. Where was he? and what was he
doing?—not only to-day, but all the days
and nights he was away from his home?
Oh Kate! Kate! does not a still, small voice
whisper to you of the share you have had in
bringing things to this state? Does it not
remind you of that evening years ago when
he you now blame so much asked you to
love him and guide him right? Oh, surely
it does, if you will only listen for a moment.

But Mrs. Gilbert gave her very little time
for reflection. She rallied her upon her
silence, and kept up a constant chit-chat,
in which Kate made an effort to join and
appear interested, which effort was seen

through, and its cause guessed at pretty
accurately by her talkative companion. As
they were passing the Park, there was a
block-up of carriages, and they were obliged
to slacken the pace they were going at for
a few moments, and, leaning forward, Mrs.
Gilbert's sharp eyes detected Lord Denton
and Captain Martin walking to and fro,
arm in arm, under the trees, away from the
general promenade. The Park had become
almost empty of its drivers and riders; the
two friends had evidently chosen a spot
where they hoped to be free from meeting
acquaintances, or having their smoke in-
terrupted in any way. They were both
laughing heartily just at the moment Mrs.
Gilbert caught sight of them.

"See, Lady Denton; there's the truant.
That is how he spends his afternoons. If I
were you, my dear, I should try to manage
him better, and put him on honour to alter
and amend his ways," said Mrs. Gilbert.

"Honour!" exclaimed Kate; "honour, indeed! I question if Lord Denton knows the true meaning of the word."

The moment she had uttered this unguarded speech, she could have bitten her tongue with anger at her stupidity. Had she silenced Mrs. Gilbert with a word or a look, as she would have done at any other moment but this, it would have certainly been better for her future peace of mind. The ice once broken, Mrs. Gilbert learned some of the inner life of her friend, and was full of condolences and advice to her.

"Oh, my dear Lady Denton, men are all alike; they want a tight rein over them, to make them feel that they can't do exactly as they please. I speak from experience, I assure you—not in my own case, for I must say poor Gilbert was a perfect lamb from the first moment he saw me; but I know what other women have to bear very often; and I say, nine times out of ten, it is their

fault for giving way so much at first. But
cheer up, and don't frown; it brings wrinkles, which are not easily got rid of, I assure
you, and do not improve your appearance."

This speech, which was meant to be very
encouraging, only added to Lady Denton's
annoyance. She was greatly relieved when
the carriage stopped at Mrs. Gilbert's door,
and she was once again alone. It was such
a relief to have no one near her—to be able
to think without interruption; and she wondered again and again at her own want of
control over her feelings. How could she
have so far forgotten what was due to herself
as to make a *confidante* of such a woman as
Mrs. Gilbert, who would, of course, talk
about it to every one? She had put herself
in her power, and must abide the conse-
quences of her indiscretion.

Kate need not have teased herself about
it so much; for her friend knew nothing

more from what she had told her than she had
guessed months before, and had frequently
spoken of it as a fact. If Kate had seen
her husband with any other of his acquaintances, she would not have felt quite as angry;
but, as her husband knew well enough, she
had such a dislike to that odious man, that
to be neglected for him was too much to
bear quietly! So she dressed for dinner,
hoping that she would not have to meet
Lord Denton. But as she went to her aunt's
room, she heard his voice in his dressing-
room, talking angrily to his valet, that made
her resolve to say nothing, or take the
slightest notice of what had occurred.

It had unfortunately happened that as he
left his house in the morning he had met
his friend, who was anxious to take him off
somewhere for an hour or two. It was an
old appointment they had promised to keep
together. Lord Denton said that he must
return to luncheon, or very soon after, and

that he must also go to Tattersall's. To
this the worthy Captain made no objection.
He would go with him there, and then there
would be plenty of time for them to go the
short distance he proposed.

So it was settled that they should try to
make all the haste they could, and combine
the two things; and off they started in a
Hansom. But, alas! time flies. It was
more than two o'clock before they left Gros-
venor Place; some other man they had arranged to see there had kept them waiting,
and so engrossed and taken up with the
subject of horses and their value and merits
was Lord Denton, he never gave one
moment's thought to his wife and home.
Away they drove from there, eagerly talking over the morning's work, Captain Martin
taking great care not to remind his friend
that he ought to have been driving the other
way. Not till he was saying good-bye to
the Captain on the Club steps did the remem-

brance of what he ought to have done flash
through his mind.

"Gad!" he exclaimed, "I've forgotten
Kate. What a confounded nuisance!"

He sprang hastily down the steps, not
waiting to hear another word, jumped into
his cab, and told the man to drive sharp.
He was really sorry, and felt how angry
Kate would be—and justly so this time, at
all events. She so seldom expressed any
wish for him to take her anywhere now-a-
days. What an idiot he was, to be sure.
Martin again—always Martin, from the very
first. He never could get away from him—
he did not know how it was. But Kate need
not know that; he could tell her something
else had detained him, and he was truly
sorry for it. It only wanted a few minutes
to dinner when he arrived home, so he
hurried off to his room to make some change
in his dress, hoping, perhaps, to throw off,
with his dusty clothes, some of the shame he

felt at having to meet his wife after behaving
so ill to her.

" Conscience makes cowards of us all."
Had Lord Denton been unavoidably prevented from returning, he might have felt
sorry, but surely not ashamed. Circumstances over which we have no control may
often keep us from fulfilling our promises;
but if we offer the truth as an apology, our
friends must indeed be ill-natured not to
accept it without blaming us. He made his
excuses to his wife as he took her down to
dinner. Kate turned very red when she
heard him say what she knew to be untrue;
but she took as little notice as possible,
merely answering, " indeed," "yes" or " no"
to all he said. If her husband could have
chosen, he would very much rather she had
given way to some show of temper; it would
not have been half so hard to endure as her
icy coldness. They went to the Opera after
dinner, and as Kate took up a young lady

from a house near her own, there was nothing more said between them then. It was one of Lady Denton's favourite operas. The gifted though not beautiful woman who sang the principal character always carried Kate away from all her annoyances, and it was perhaps the place of all others where she thoroughly enjoyed herself. They left rather earlier than usual, and having set down her charge, Lady Denton was sur-. prised to find that her husband placed his arm round her waist and begged to be forgiven. All the anger of her pent-up feelings burst forth at this into the most passionate upbraidings. She started to the other side of the carriage, and told him she hated the touch of his hand. "I despise you for your cowardly attempt to deceive me. I know who you were with to-day. I saw you in the Park. Do you remember who and what I am, sir? How dare you insult me, and palm me off with false words?"

She bounded out of the carriage, and was in her own room before he had given his hat and coat to the man-servant. He felt perfectly stupefied. How dreadfully fierce she looked as the lights flashed on her face; she almost seemed like a goddess of wrath and vengeance. Was there ever such an unlucky dog in the whole wide world as he? How cruel Fate was to him! He didn't mention Martin to Kate, because he knew if he had she would have been annoyed at his doing so. And then to think of her seeing them. "What a horrid bore it was." He sat and solaced himself with cigars and brandy-and-water, thinking over the scene in the carriage, and repeated to himself all that Kate had said, till his brain became too muddled to have any very clear ideas, past or present; and when he did move to retire, he could scarcely drag himself upstairs to take the rest and sleep he so much needed.

Norah had followed Lady Denton to her

room, and turned the key at her mistress's bidding. Kate's first inquiry was for her aunt, and she was pleased to hear that she had had a nice sleep, and was considerably better. As Norah brushed out the long black hair, and saw Kate's face before her in the glass, she could not help being struck with the look of weariness, and asked to be allowed to fetch her a little wine.

" No, Norah, I will take nothing to-night; my head is almost bursting now, and wine will not improve it, I fear," replied her mistress.

" You look so pale and ill," said Norah, pityingly. She was very much struck with the difference, because as a rule Kate was in her brightest mood when she returned from the Opera.

" I confess to a good deal of heartache as well as headache, Norah; but I shall be better in the morning, I dare say."

" Ah! dear; ah! dear," said Norah; " I

little thought I should ever see you like this, darlint. Your bonny face is altered since you left the ould home. Thank God! the master didn't live to see it. It would have killed him entirely, I warrant."

It must be remembered that Norah had known and loved Lady Denton all her life. She looked upon her almost as a child of her own, having taken her when her mother died, and devoted herself to her, though she was very little more than a child herself at the time ; and of course she saw no fault in her, and was ready to blame any one who caused her a moment's uneasiness. The feeling she had for Lord Denton was certainly not love or anything akin to it, and she was often tempted to quarrel in a mild form with poor Miss Casteldi for not always agreeing with her. In mentioning her father, Norah had struck a chord which vibrated through and through her mistress's heart. She wept bitter tears long after the faithful Norah had retired to rest, and she also felt thankful that her poor father had been spared the misery of knowing that his well-beloved child was a neglected, unhappy wife.

CHAPTER VII.

THE next day was brighter than any one could have hoped or expected. Miss Casteldi was so much better, that she came down to breakfast, and there were letters from friends, — one from Mrs. Leigh in answer to Kate's begging for a visit before the season was over. Mrs. Leigh disliked railway travelling so much that she scarcely ever took a journey but for health's sake, and she declined for herself, but half promised Helen should come.

"Both of us, my dear Kate, are, as usual, you will say, very busy," wrote Mrs. Leigh; "and though we long to see you, we would

rather so much it were here we did so, as
your long absences distress us, after your
having held out such hopes of our seeing so
much of you at Denton. Are you intending
to come in the autumn if all is well? I feel
almost inclined to refuse Helen to you if you
are not. But this would be selfish, however;
so I must say if Helen can and will come to
you I have really no objection to make. I
have no doubt she will enjoy some of the
gaiety and change you offer her, and have
no fear that it will unsettle her or make her
discontented with her quiet country life."

A short note from Helen followed this, in
which she named the day of her coming to
London.

Kate was very pleased. She had not seen
her for so long, and Helen was so different
to all the women she knew in London, it
would be quite a relief to talk to her and
take her about; and many were the treats
Kate resolved to give her.

"A little dissipation will do Helen good, Aunt Neta. She stays down there from year's end to year's end, never hardly going away except to some pokey sea-side place, where she gets as brown as a gipsy, and thinks it a treat to get an old, musty, three-volume novel to read on the sands."

"Well, Kitty," replied her aunt, "she enjoys it thoroughly, I have no doubt. We don't all long after the same kind of thing. She fills up her time with something more substantial than mere worldly amusements, out of which there is very little lasting enjoyment to be got."

"Now please, Aunt Neta, if you love me, don't begin to be moral. I can't listen to it to-day of all days. Wait till Helen comes; you will have a ready and sympathetic listener in her. She likes it, I know,—I never did."

For the evening of the day on which Helen was to arrive, Lady Denton had

issued invitations for a dance, thinking it
would be the best way of introducing her
to some of her fashionable acquaintances.
Helen came rather late in the afternoon,
was tired, and wanted to excuse herself
and go to bed, but Kate would not hear
of such a thing for a moment. "Go to
bed, you little rebel," she exclaimed, kissing
her, "how very absurd and childish. I am
giving this dance expressly for you. I want
to show you to my friends, and you must
be dutiful and grateful, and look your best
to please me, Nellie, love. A fresh country
beauty is a novelty at the end of the season,
so take your coffee and rest for a couple of
hours or more after dinner; if you like you
need not come down before eleven. I will
come for you when I am ready. Adieu
for the present." Helen lay on her sofa,
closed her eyes, and thought how very
much her friend had altered; not so much
in appearance as in manner — she seemed

to have lost that repose they had all so much admired her for having, and was more restless and demonstrative to her. This may have been occasioned by the pleasure she felt at seeing her again, or it was, perhaps, the way with people who were obliged to be fashionable,—they put on unnatural manners very often, said Helen to herself. Lady Denton peeped into Helen's room, and brought some flowers for her hair, and expressed her satisfaction at her appearance. As the night wore on the rooms became very crowded; dancing went on in spite of that inconvenience till late in the following morning, when Helen retired, fairly done up.

"Now confess, Nellie, haven't you enjoyed yourself immensely? You have had some splendid dancing partners, haven't you?"

"Oh, yes I have, thank you. It has been so pleasant, I own Kate; but, dear me, much of this would kill me very soon. I am

dreadfully tired, and it is very late. I ought
to be getting up now."

"Oh, nonsense, Helen; I often come home
by daylight. The more one does, the more
one is able to do, I find, and 'the more the
merrier!' is still my motto. But I won't
detain you longer. Get to bed, you sweet
little innocent! May your repose be refreshing, and your dreams of—" She closed the
door, and Helen did not catch the last word.

There was so much to be seen and done,
and so very little time to do it in, that Helen
had scarcely a moment to call her own. Kate
took her everywhere, and Lord Denton was
very attentive and anxious for her to enjoy
herself thoroughly. Mrs. Gilbert invited her
to an evening at her house, but Kate decided
to accept something else instead, which Mrs.
Gilbert was not pleased at. However, she
kept that to herself, although she felt Kate
had purposely avoided bringing Helen into
contact with her; but she had good reason

for keeping friendly with Lady Denton, therefore pocketed the affront quietly.

Lady Denton could not persuade Helen to ride with her in London, so she had driven with her in the mornings; but she was longing for a good canter, she told Helen, and thought she must go to the Row.

"Now do, Helen, try Freeda; she is as quiet as a lamb. You could not, if you wished even, come to any harm on her."

"No, Kate, thank you. I really should be nervous and frightened on anything with four legs. I always did spoil your rides somehow, even in our quiet country roads. You go though without me, and I will drive with your aunt and take a chair. You can deign to notice me if you see me looking on."

Kate was not long before she had started off, and was enjoying the fresh air and the less crowded road. As yet there were comparatively few lady riders there. She bowed.

to several acquaintances who passed her, and
if she had given a glance at the loiterers on the
promenade, she would have seen some one she
had known very intimately in happier days.
As it was, she passed quite close to the railing
against which he was leaning; but she was
smiling and nodding to a little child on a
pony the other side of her. He was tall and
dark, rather foreign-looking, and evidently a
stranger. He recognized Lady Denton, or
thought he did, for he followed a few steps
behind her, to make assurance doubly sure.
He had been idly killing time, tossing his
cane about in a listless sort of way, wondering if he should see any one he knew.
At first he thought he would cross over, and
see her return on the other side; but he
altered his mind, and went out of the Park,
back to his hotel in Piccadilly. Had he
gone across, as he first intended, he would
have seen more old friends, who would have
given him a warm welcome back to Eng-

land. Kate was in wonderfully good spirits
when she drew up to speak to Helen, who
stood at arm's-length, admiring her horse.

That same evening they went to the
Opera, to hear the 'Trovatore.' The house
was full of youthful and beautiful listeners.
Helen had been looking round it with her
glass, between the scenes, when suddenly
she seized Kate's hand, leaned forward to
her, and said, breathlessly,—

"Look, Kate; look opposite, to the right!
There is Bartle Blake in that box. I am
quite certain he is there; at the corner,
half hid by the curtain."

"My dear Helen, don't agitate yourself
about it so much. I dare say you are right;
but why you should be so surprised I can't
imagine."

"Oh, because I had not an idea of his
being over here. But, look, Kate; do,
now; isn't it him? Can you see where I
mean?"

"Oh, yes, quite well; there is no doubt
about the identity. He seems to be far too
much engrossed with the girls in that box to
notice you. But don't distress yourself,
Nellie; I will take care you meet him somewhere before you go away."

"I wish he would look this way, and that
I could catch his eye. I wonder if he can
have written to mamma, and she has forgotten to mention it to me? If he is going
there, I must return at once."

"Well, Nellie, you can't possibly go at
this present moment; so you may as well
listen to this delicious air," Kate answered;
"it is one of my favourites."

She might have added, and of our friend
opposite too. As the gifted singer, in a
clear rich voice, gave "Non ti scordar di
me," the hot blood rushed through Kate's
veins, crimsoning her face and neck. A
moment afterwards she was deadly pale.
Oh, how those words brought back to her,

as if it had been only yesterday, the last
evening she had heard it in her own happy
home, when everything was well with her.
Then came, following quickly, the parting on
the steamer, the few days at The Ridgway,
the scene at St. Albans, when Bartle had
told her how very dearly he loved her. She
had thrown all this away,—for what? "Rank
and wealth," conscience whispered; "and
misery," she added herself.

Helen, who had scarcely taken her eyes
away from the box opposite, was rewarded,
at last, by receiving a low bow from the
gentleman in return for hers. Lady Denton
had placed herself so much in shadow that
it was impossible for him to see who Helen's
companion was. He may have guessed, perhaps, because if it had been Mrs. Leigh she
would have bowed too, he knew.

" Those girls are strangers, Helen; I have
not seen them before that I remember; and,
as they are in the Russian Ambassador's box,

I dare say they are some people Mr. Blake has got to know over there, and they are taking a little notice of him." Lady Denton said this with a slight curl of her lip.

"Notice indeed, Kate! Whoever they are, I am sure they may be proud of knowing such a man," replied Helen, indignantly.

The entrance of the subject of their conversation prevented Kate replying. Helen welcomed him very warmly, asked him many questions which she hardly waited to have answered, and Kate sat looking as indifferent as if he had been a total stranger to her. She shook hands when he came in, and only joined in the conversation with a "Yes" or "No," and a smile occasionally at Helen's enthusiasm. It was so unlike Helen to show any amount of excess of pleasure at anything, that Lady Denton was very much struck with her evident delight at seeing their old friend, and thought she had never seen Helen look so pretty and so animated before.

In answer to Mr. Blake's inquiry after her husband, Lady Denton assured him he was quite well, and would be very glad to see him if he would call, and told him their address.

"I can't ensure his being at home any day, but of course, as Helen is with us, you won't be dreadfully disappointed if he is not there, I dare say. To-morrow is my afternoon at home, when you will be more likely to find him than any other day."

Helen asked who the young ladies were opposite.

"Two sisters of my most intimate friend," replied Mr. Blake; "this is their first visit to London. I shall be most happy to introduce them to you; the younger one sings beautifully, and that has thrown us a good deal together. In fact, I spend most of my evenings at their house; they are all most kind and hospitable to me."

Before he left the box, Lord Denton came

in. He had not the remotest idea who his
wife's visitor was. Kate explained, and then
he remembered to have met him at the
Clennings' "ages ago," he said, and cordially welcomed him, hoping to see him
again.

No words can tell what Lady Denton
suffered that night. This was almost worse
than anything that had yet happened to her.
Why did he come there, and talk to her of
his happiness, prosperity, and friends? She
neither cared to see them nor hear him talk
about them. What were they to her? How
little he seemed to care to notice or talk to
her now. Time was when to be near her
was perfect happiness to him, and he found
it difficult to pay even common attention to
any other lady when she was by; when a
look or a word from her would have made
him a willing prisoner at her side for any
length of time, and under any circumstances,
but now he hurried in and hurried out, after

·just the commonplace interchange of civilities between them.

"After all," she said to herself, "I am alone to blame for all this. Whatever he feels now, he *did* love me once, I know, and I—. Ah, well, she would not dream of that even; she must school her heart, and her face, to meet and greet him as a friend."

Helen chatted all the way home with Lord Denton. Kate complained of heat and felt tired, and she leaned back in the carriage and closed her eyes.

"Good-night, Kate; God bless you!" said Helen. "I hope your head will be better to-morrow. Weren't you pleased to see Bartle Blake again, and wasn't he looking splendid?"

Helen returned home thoroughly satisfied with all she had seen or done. She had almost persuaded Lord and Lady Denton to come there instead of going to the Continent, as they were half inclined to do. Kate did not promise faithfully; she could not make up her mind so long before the time, and she did not intend to leave town till the very end of the season. "She so infinitely preferred London to any other place in the world," she said.

"Kate is very much altered, mamma; and Lord Denton is ever so much stouter than he was. He has a high colour, too, and does not appear to have very good health. I am sure a quiet winter here would do them both all the good in the world; but, although he liked the idea of coming, Kate would not decide. She is more wilful than ever, and is constantly out and about everywhere night and day."

CHAPTER VIII.

ATE had made no more con-
fidential disclosures to Mrs. Gilbert,
and had really seen very little of
her during Helen's stay. As Captain
Martin was a frequent visitor at
her house in the evening, she had to caution
him, and make him promise not to attempt
to come in when Etienne told him that his
mistress was not at home, because then there
were people there whom she did not wish him
to see, as they were not on very friendly
terms with him, and, without mentioning
any names, Captain Martin was given to
understand that Lady Denton was as fond
of play as she was of admiration. He eagerly

caught at the idea of his being able some future day to use his information to her discredit and annoyance. He was morally certain that her husband did not dream of her doing anything of the kind; and if he could he would find out, in an indirect way, what he would do if he did get to know. He would talk it over again with Mrs. Gilbert, and be quite certain about it, and then—

"Ah, then! my Lady Denton, we shall see what then."

So this Lord of the Creation indulged in future visions of how he would humble, and bring low with galling vexation, a woman whose greatest injury to him had been not allowing herself to be intimate or friendly with him, and who had presumed to show him that his society was distasteful to her. Mrs. Gilbert was positive no one knew Kate came to her so often. She never breathed it to any one. This was true in most cases, but she and the Captain were on very intimate terms with each other, and had so many interests in common, that "telling him was only like knowing herself," she said.

One evening, soon after Helen had gone, Kate drove to Mrs. Gilbert's from the theatre, and sat there a long time losing the contents of her well-filled purse at one stake. This only added fuel to the flame; she went on, on, utterly reckless whether she won or lost. She had learned to love this more than any other of her amusements, and gave her whole ideas to it while under its fascination. To Kate's intense surprise, Captain Martin came into the room where they were sitting, and started back with well-feigned surprise when he saw her, making some familiar remark upon her ill luck, and smiling. If a look could have annihilated him, he would have ended there and then his existence, which perhaps no one would have regretted; but he managed to survive it, although he could not keep his eyes on her proud face as she rose from the table, and declared to Mrs. Gilbert, "She could not breathe in such company." She ordered Etienne to fetch a cab in a tone of voice which made him move quickly, and open his sleepy eyes, wondering what had happened to ruffle her ladyship. Mrs. Gilbert followed, and tried to pour heaps of contrite excuses in her ear, declaring that her servant should suffer for this. Captain Martin thoroughly enjoyed Lady Denton's discomfiture; he knew that she would rather a thousand times the earth had opened and swallowed her up than be seen in such company by him. He knew she did feel it acutely in spite of her high air and scorn of him. The two men who were there took no notice of the *rencontre*, beyond saying they were sorry Lady Denton had left so abruptly. Captain Martin knew that, once in their toils, nothing but a miracle could save Kate from utter ruin. So he determined this should be his excuse for telling

Lord Denton of some of Lady Denton's goings-on. He took his first opportunity of having his friend alone about a week afterwards to tell him, which he did with every appearance of interest and sorrow for Lady Denton.

"You know what Mrs. Gilbert is as well as I can tell you, but you don't know Vavasour and Trelling; they are fellows even I would scarcely cut a card with, and will fleece her of every penny she has before she is aware of it."

Lord Denton was completely taken by surprise. He at first was inclined to declare it was untrue, but there was something so serious in the Captain's manner that it was impossible not to believe he was speaking truly. He could scarcely reply to what the Captain had said, and what he did say was confused and vague enough.

He pictured to himself how thoroughly altered Kate was to have been seen in such company. His proud, peerless Kate, as he used to call her, in close company with two of the most notorious gamblers he knew in the whole world! Come what might, he resolved to tell her of what he had heard, and forbid the repetition of such doings. Late that night he went into his wife's room, with noisy impatience, determining to have an explanation with her.

"Leave the room, Norah," he said; "I wish to speak to her Ladyship alone."

As Norah turned to obey, Lady Denton said, not moving off her chair, and hardly looking off the French novel she had been reading,—

"Stay, Norah. Whatever Lord Denton has to say he can say it before you; in fact, I would rather he did. I do not wish to be left alone with him in his present excited state."

As Lord Denton was moving uneasily about in the room, she turned and said, mockingly,—

"Now, my Lord, I am quite ready to listen. What have you to say to me of such importance that you intrude yourself at this late hour in my room ?"

This must have been exceedingly aggravating to her husband. A most angry scene took place between them. His patiently-borne trials of her utter neglect and scorn made him give vent to expressions which were more like what one might expect from a man bereft of his senses than a rational human being.

Of course Kate knew who had been his informant. She had almost expected something of this kind to happen. She did not attempt to defend or excuse herself against his, alas ! too true accusations till he hinted about his money going in that way, and commanded her to tell him what she had lost at play. She rose from her chair, and indignantly refused to reply to such insolence.

" Have done, sir, and leave my room immediately. Here, at least, I have a right to be free from your odious presence. You are not fit to come near any one in your present condition. The fumes of wine have already filled the room. Go, sir, I say, or I will ring the servants up to you."

Having said all and more than he at first intended, and not wishing to prolong the painful scene, he turned on his heel and did her bidding, muttering some half-audible sentences.

Norah was in an agony of grief. It was something so awful for her to witness. She trembled with fear, and cried bitterly. Kate, on the other hand, was exceedingly angry. "How dare he tax her with spending his money, when she had never gone one penny beyond what she was perfectly able to pay out of her own private income? It was so mean and so utterly untrue; so despicable of him to mention it even if it had been true; unpardonable as it was not.

But she would put an end to all this. She
began to fear that some time or other he
would force himself into her presence in a
worse state than he was to-night, and who
knew what dreadful thing might happen?
She would no longer subject herself to such
shameful coarse expressions and scenes. Come
what might, she would not stay longer in
that house or under any roof shared with Lord
Denton. She would make up her mind and
go somewhere soon, and then he could do as
he pleased without any consideration for her.
She had feared for a long while past that,
sooner or later, it would come to this ; and to-
night's bitter experience convinced her that
the time had come for her to take steps to
ensure herself some future peace of mind and
safety. Her very heart seemed to revolt at
the bare idea of coming in contact with him
again. What should she do, and to whom
should she go to ask advice ? Not Aunt
Neta, she was so nervous and fearful, and so

inclined to blame her for whatever went
wrong. She could not explain to her nor
make her understand the state he was in.
She would only cry, and beg her to let her
speak to her husband, which, of course, there
would be no use in her doing, or any good
result from it. She could not and would not
tell Mrs. Leigh or Helen, although she immediately thought of them in her difficulty.

It would have been a relief to pour out her
wrongs to Mrs. Leigh; but now, above all
times, when she was expecting guests, she
could nottrouble her. Besides, would not
every one think as Miss Casteldi did, that
she had better stay and try to mend matters?
Of course they would, she decided to herself,
so there was no plan better than to arrange
her private affairs quickly and go right away.
She would leave a letter for Lord Denton and
one for her aunt too, and would assure the
latter that she should know of her movements
when she had found some place where she

could resolve to stay, and also that, if her
aunt cared to join her, she would only be too
glad to have her with her anywhere. She
sat up a long time thinking and planning,
and the most satisfactory conclusion she
came to was to keep to her first idea, and
hasten away as soon as she could. At last,
worn out but not sleepy, she went to bed,
but "kind Nature's sweet restorer" would
not come to refresh her weary mind. She
lay and read, and turned, and tossed about
till it was quite broad daylight, when she
fell into an uneasy slumber, and forgot for a
few short hours her anxiety and difficulties.

That same evening, at Mrs. Leigh's
house, a far different and much pleasanter
scene took place. Mr. Blake was staying
there, according to promise, and was accompanied by his friend Mr. Nitikin. The two
young sisters were to come for a few days
later on, and then they were going to make
a tour through Ireland and Scotland, taking

the former first, as Mr. Blake, knowing the country so well, would be an invaluable guide to them.

Mrs. Leigh and Bartle found plenty to do with talking over all his plans, and Helen was learning some new game of cards from the young Russian. A large party of our old friends were asked to meet Mrs. Leigh's guests. They are almost all the same as we have seen there before some years ago : Mr. and Mrs. Clayton, who were both much frailer; Mr. and Mrs. Clenning, their son, and daughters Julia and Annie, Captain and Mrs. Mylett (Mary Clenning that used to be). Mrs. Clenning looked wonderfully strong and well, considering that she was still a martyr to constant aches and pains, such as no one else in this wide world had ever endured before; and Mr. Clenning looked as good-tempered and genial as usual. He, too, had a few stray grey hairs to show that Time leaves marks even on the happiest heads and faces. Captain and Mrs. Mylett were on a visit to her parents with their two little girls, who were an inexhaustible fund of amusement and interest to grandpapa and aunties. Mrs. Clenning was puzzled, she often said, to see her husband dance so much attendance on such very small children. She had not an idea how he could bear it, for the least noise from them always made her head fit to burst. She had never been thoroughly satisfied with Mary's marriage, and could find something to regret about it even now. She was so sorry her grand-children were girls, she said. What would they do if they had a large family of them? It would require an immense fortune to bring them up and marry them. She would, in all probability, have said just the same if they had been boys, for whatever really happened and could not be helped, Mrs. Clenning always wished it were different. It was a matter of grave regret that Julia and Annie

were still unmarried. They were getting
on, and there was no time to lose, she felt;
but they were too particular, she often said
to her friends. This was not strictly true,
for neither of them had had an opportunity
of refusing any one; still it pleased their
mother to talk as if half the county had
been at their feet, and no one cared to
try to prove to her that she was wrong.
However, if report spoke truly, the fair
and still good-looking Julia was soon to
become engaged, and, as a natural consequence of that, we may suppose married to
an Hon. and Rev. T. Templar, of excellent
blood and expectations, a man of about her
own age, with agreeable manners and a
pleasant face. He was one of the guests at
The Ridgway, and let us hope, poor man!
that no jealous revilings were raised in his
breast at the very flattering attentions he
had to witness paid to his lady-love by Mr.
Nitikin. It was very natural that they

should all talk and think of Lady Denton,
and wonder where she was that evening.
They all agreed in thinking that she would
have liked to be one of their party.

"I am very sorry the Dentons are away
from the Court; it is such a lovely house.
I should have liked you to have seen it, and
Lady Denton gives such splendid parties.
We miss her so much," said Annie Clenning
to Miss Olga Nitikin.

"I dare say you do, but I really did not
think her quite as charming as I hear every
one say she is. My brother admires her
very much indeed. Neither my sister nor
myself took a great fancy to her. We
thought her so very icy in manner."

"A good many people say the same thing,
I know, but it is a great mistake. She is
proud at first, I dare say; that is only manner
though, and it wears off very quickly. If you
had seen more of her, you would have been
sure to allow that she is very charming."

Miss Nitikin looked very much as if she would have liked to have said that under any circumstances she could never have agreed with Annie, but she was too polite to say so to her. Very possibly Lady Denton did not care to unbend or make a favourable impression on the girl who was now receiving all the numberless attentions that were once given only to her. However, Lady Denton was mistaken in her surmises, for Mrs. Leigh, while talking over Mr. Blake's affairs with him, found out that there was nothing particular ever likely to be between them. He admired Olga very much indeed, so he did her sister: they were nice girls, he said, and had been very kind to him—they were very good friends, and he hoped they always would be, but anything else was not to be thought of nor mentioned.

CHAPTER IX.

RS. GILBERT made many attempts to see Lady Denton, and make her peace with her; but she had not succeeded in either finding her at home or meeting her anywhere. She was really as sorry about it as she could be about any misfortune which could happen to any one but herself; and although she had given the Captain a kind of permission to come in "some" night when her Ladyship was there, she had not anticipated his doing so so soon. She made a great show of anger and resentment to Captain Martin, and vented her rage and ill humour thoroughly upon her luckless man-

servant: not that he cared two straws for
what his mistress said to him, especially in
the way of scolding; he was so thoroughly
used to it that he scarcely listened to her.
Lady Denton determined, if possible, not to
see her again; and Mrs. Gilbert, after being
refused admittance several times with "Not
at home," when she was morally certain it
was only a put-off, waged war again with
the Captain for making such a stupid blunder
and frightening her prey away. But they
soon became friends again—probably she was
consoled with the Captain holding out hopes
of a fresh victim for her at no very distant
period; in the mean time it suited Mrs. Gilbert
not to be too severe or vindictive.

London was again fast thinning: the Row
was comparatively deserted by its fair riders;
chairs began to be collected into large piles
under the trees, turned one on the other;
nurses and children had decidedly gone in
great numbers to some cooler, fresher places,

where many of the latter were indulging in the freedom of the sea-side or country life, —spending hours with the sand and shells, their little spades and pails doing good service, and giving great pleasure; while others, perhaps, were playing with equal freedom and delight in shady lanes and well-wooded parks. Many fathers and mothers, and other members of the grown-up fashionable community, were resting from their labours, and preparing for the quieter country season.

Lord Denton had signified his intention of leaving London on a certain day. He intended to go straight to Denton Court, he said, and Kate had offered no opposition to his plans. Not one word had passed between them referring to that last sad night when he had so thoroughly lost all control over himself. Miss Casteldi was extremely pleased at the idea of going home, as she called it, and was very busy making her pre-

parations for the flitting. Kate was busy
too; it was their last day in town, and the
last day she intended staying under her
husband's roof. She had made her arrangements to go some distance on the journey
with them, and stay for a few days' visit
with some old friends of her father's, whom
Lord Denton had declined to go to then, as
he wished to be at his own place, he said.
But he thought Kate could go alone; and
from there she intended either to go over to
Ireland or back to London,—which plan she
would take she was not quite decided about.

She was very busy writing letters, reading
over old ones, and burning some of them;
looking over her jewellery and her accounts.
Had any one seen her making everything so
neat and compact, they must have wondered
why she was paying so much attention to such
matters when she had a clever, willing maid
to do her bidding. Some tiny notes lay on
her desk which she had looked at several

times as if she could not quite make up her
mind what to do with them ; but ultimately
they shared the fate of the rest, and were
torn up in pieces and thrown into a basket
at hand. She then turned her attention to
her banker's book, and found that her balance
there was very small. But then she had no
bills to pay. She always had made it a rule
never to go on month after month with bills
due to tradespeople. She had learned from
her father to be prompt and punctual in
money matters, and had not fallen into the
habit so general now-a-days of running in
debt for any length of time.

May we venture here to remark, without
wishing to give offence to our lady readers,
that very many of the failures, and much of
the ruin among our tradespeople, would
never take place if they could get in their
bills? If ladies would only buy what they
can afford to pay for, and do so when they
purchase, it would be better and kinder

We have often wondered how women of refined education and good birth can attire
themselves, as so many do, in costly dresses
and adornments which they are in debt for
to, we will say, a well-to-do tradesman or
merchant, knowing full well that they cannot
really afford to pay for them till the articles
are perhaps worn out and cast aside, or till
they are dunned out of their disgraceful debts.
The poorer woman would, nine cases out of
ten, be too proud to follow her aristocratic
sisters' example, even if she had the opportunity. But this is not keeping to our story.

Lady Denton had not taken even Norah
into her confidence; she thought it wisest to
leave her in doubt. She must have bound
her to keep it secret, and that was distasteful
to her, although she knew that Norah would
follow her willingly to the end of the earth if
she wished it. So Norah wondered "what"
her mistress was going to do: that she intended something strange she felt certain, for

never before had she seen her so quiet and
still, and so taken up with her packing
arrangements.

Lady Denton felt very depressed while
dressing for dinner, and wondered if, after
all, she would waver at the last. How glad
she was not to be going anywhere after
dinner! She would have a quiet evening
with her aunt, and sing to and amuse her,
if she could. Perhaps all she had done had
tired her, and made her feel weary : she
would try not to appear so; and went downstairs determining to throw the feeling off, if
possible.

But though she sang and talked to her
aunt, she could scarcely keep herself from own-
ing to her that she was dreadfully wretched.
Lord Denton had not returned to dinner.
He had said when he went out in the morning that very likely he would not do so.
He came back to say this to Kate, who was
reading the *Times*, which made her look up

and wonder why he had thought it necessary
to tell her. It was a usual thing for him
to stay away and not say a word about it.
She several times during the day fancied
she could hear him saying, as he stood door
in hand, " Good-bye, Kate; don't wait
dinner for me," to which she replied with
a bend of her head, as she thought it something what he used to do before they drifted
so far apart.

About ten o'clock that evening a few
gentlemen were sitting in a rather small
luxuriantly-furnished room in The Albany.
The host was Captain Martin. They all
appeared to have been dining together, and
apparently intended to finish the evening in
a very jovial manner. One or two were
lazily lolling in the large easy-chairs, another
on a sofa, while they all seemed more or less
in need of sleep, if one might judge from
their indolent attitudes. Large and small
decanters and bottles were on the table, with

some boxes which contained what was to form the amusement of the evening. They were all smoking. Clouds of smoke filled the room, and no one seemed to object to it. Then some one started a conversation, which caused peals of loud laughter from the listeners.

Captain Martin had been sitting on the opposite side of the table to Lord Denton. He leaned forward and made some remark (in reference to the joke they had just heard) in a half kind of whisper, when his Lordship, who was in the act of drinking something out of a tumbler, sprang up and sent the contents of the glass in the Captain's face, exclaiming, as he did so, between his teeth, "Liar." He made a hurried movement as if to go round to the other side, when he caught his foot in the rug, which his chair-leg had misplaced, and fell heavily forward, bringing the side of his head on to the sharp edge of the fender. Blood flowed freely. He lay quite still and apparently dead.

Fear was on every face. They all threw aside their pipes and cigars, and were on their feet immediately. Captain Martin, wiping his blinded eyes, sobered at the sight before him, looked the astonishment he could not utter. So suddenly had it happened, that it was simply impossible to make out the cause of it. No one had heard distinctly what had passed between them; some said one thing, some another. The Captain was most surprised and puzzled of all, as he hadn't dreamt of giving any offence.

They got some help; one of them rushed for the nearest doctor, and the Captain's man-servant suggested that they had better lift him on to the bed in the next room. He was not a light burden, and surely if any appalling sight could make their hearts sink within them, that one before them must indeed have had that effect. Two or three of them went away. They saw there were too many to be of any use. The others were anxiously awaiting the coming of the medical man, who said, when he came, that Lord Denton had had a fit, and he could not yet tell how it would terminate. He was not dead, that he assured them, which was a great relief to hear.

Some one suggested sending for Lady Denton. Who should go to her? Could he be taken home if they waited a little, or would it be safe to leave it till morning before they let her know? The doctor was too much taken up with the patient for them to put the question to him. He found Lord Denton had lost a deal of blood, and it was some time before he showed any signs of consciousness. He lay perfectly still, with every vestige of colour gone out of his usually flushed face; and when he sighed deeply, and made an uneasy movement of the head, Captain Martin breathed more freely, and asked the doctor if he would do. He had suffered agonies in the last hour or two. How unpleasant it would have been if Denton had died there so suddenly, he thought. These things were always dreadfully exaggerated; he couldn't have stopped people from talking and wondering. It would have brought him into no end of trouble and annoyance. As it was, there would be plenty of fuss made, no doubt.

No feeling of remorse, no pity, no shame, no thought or care for his friend's sufferings, or of his being launched into eternity without a moment's warning, entered the Captain's head for a moment; the first surprise over, he could think of nothing but the inconvenience it would have been to him. The doctor said, in reply to the question about his being moved, that it was quite impossible to do it yet, and he thought that Lady Denton had better be sent for, late as it was.

Who would go and tell her? Captain
Martin said he could not; some one else said
he would rather not; then a third offered to
be the bearer of the sad news, for, as he said,
some one must do it, and there was no use
delaying. It was not any delicacy of feeling
or refinement which caused the Captain to
decline: he had not the courage to face the
woman on whom he had helped to bring
this trouble. Besides, he said aloud,—"I had
better stay and watch Denton; I may be of
use to him, you know; and be sure you ask
her to send his man at once."

Lady Denton and Miss Casteldi had retired to their rooms about eleven o'clock.
As they bade each other good-night in the
drawing-room, Miss Casteldi said "she supposed George would soon be home." Kate
lingered a few minutes afterwards, giving
some slight directions to the footman as she
gathered her thimble and scissors into her
work-basket. She felt she would have liked

to stay up all night; she dreaded going to her room. Why was this oppression weighing her down so low? But it was silly to linger, and give way. She wished she could hear that her husband was in; he had been scarcely out of her mind all day, although she had done so much, and been so full of other thoughts too.

As Norah brushed her hair, silent tears fell fast on the white hands in her lap. Oh, those blessed tears!—silent emblems of sadness, but also sure signs with Kate of subdued better feelings gaining ground, and bringing with them remnants of purer, holier thoughts not quite dead. She had not retired long when she heard several voices near her door. Then Norah gave a sudden exclamation which Kate heard, and she sprang out of bed, opened her door, demanding to know what was wrong. A gentleman was in his master's room downstairs waiting to see her. His Lordship was not well, he

believed, the man said, very reluctant to
be the bearer of such news. Lady Denton
was very much respected by her servants,
and they would any of them have been glad
to spare her pain or trouble. Hastily dressing herself, with Norah's trembling fingers to
help her, Lady Denton and her aunt went
down to hear what was wrong.

"I really do not think there is any cause
to alarm yourselves; I did not come away
till your husband was recovering, but the
doctor advised your being sent for. I am
sorry to have brought such a sad message.
Can I be of any use? My cab is at the
door; if that would hasten your getting
there, I shall be glad if you will accept it."

Kate's trembling limbs would hardly support her as she listened. The young man
pitied her, and thought how she must love
her husband to be so agitated and confused,
and how mistaken people were who believed
that they were an unhappy couple. He had

seen Lady Denton before, had been introduced
to her in a gay assembly, and he thought
her very lovely then, but not to be compared
to what she seemed now to him, with her
troubled white face, full of (as he thought)
tender love and wifely anxiety. Her visitor
bowed in reply to her assurance that they
would follow him very quickly, and that
they would gladly accept the offer of the use
of his cab. Miss Casteldi would not hear of
her niece going alone to her husband. She
insisted upon accompanying her, although
she agreed with Kate that she could be of
little use to him, while he was in his present
unconscious state, and away from his own
home.

CHAPTER X.

ADY DENTON'S appearance at Captain Martin's room was a very great surprise to him. She passed him without saying a single sentence, asking the man-servant, who had let her in and followed her silently upstairs, to show her where Lord Denton was. The doctor rose up from the chair by the bed-side as she entered, and offered it to her. He explained in a few whispered sentences what had happened, and what had better be done for the patient, who was just then sleeping, and would be more benefited by that than anything else they could do for him. Extreme quiet was absolutely necessary, and constant attention to the bandages being

kept wet and cold. There was no help for
it; lie there he must for a few days, at
least; and Lady Denton remained too, Norah
coming to be with her when Miss Casteldi
went away for a time.

They moved him, as soon as they could,
to his own house, where he lay for days,
sometimes hardly noticing anything or any
one around him. Sometimes, when he moved
his aching head restlessly and moaned, Kate,
who sat and watched and waited, would lean
over him, and whisper in his ear; then he
would open his eyes, look vacantly at her,
and smile mournfully. At other times, he
would appear to notice her and her aunt,
and look pleased to see them near him.

Almost his first expressed wish was to be
taken to Denton Court, and they managed
to take him there after a little, without
any apparent fatigue or harm. He was not
going on quite as satisfactorily as the doctors
would have liked he should. His mind was

much weakened, it was very evident, although he was able to talk and listen; but he did not gain strength nor recover the use of his leg and arm, which were stiff and painful every now and then. The wound in his head had healed to all appearance, and he suffered scarcely any pain there.

Where were all Lady Denton's plans? Ah, where indeed! Did she think of them as she moved about the silent house, and watched in the same room where she had lain a few years before in so much danger? Did she regret the unfortunate differences that had so long divided them? Ah, yes! indeed she did.

How his pale, wan face reproached her silently, and brought back to her memory all her neglected duties, his patient forbearance for so long, his ready willingness to give way to her till she had worn out his temper, and she feared his love, and driven him from her into the companionship of

those who had led him into excesses, and
with whom he had nearly lost his life. Oh,
the miserable, mistaken past! what would
she not have given to have been able to blot
the remembrance of it out for ever! How
she went back to the time when she had
been so ill, and remembered it as she had
never done before. All his untiring devotion, day and night; his extreme thankfulness when he was allowed to see her for a
few moments; how he carried her in his
strong arms from one room to the other
when she was weak and helpless—he so
glad and happy to see her improve every
day.

She might well think of all this, and
lament over the poor return she had made.
Only too surely did remorse follow her,
and fill her heart with sadness and reproof.
How she resolved to try and redeem the
past. She would do her duty, and show
him how sorry she was for all that had

happened. How thankful she was that circumstances had obliged her not to hurry away from his home and protection, and go where possibly she would have been no happier nor more contented. How mercifully her plans had been frustrated; and, thank Heaven, no one knew of them. How she prayed for guidance and help in her great need, and became more anxious every day that her husband did not improve.

Mrs. Leigh and Helen came constantly to see and help her, and lent her their old valuable maid, who was a capital sick-nurse, to fill the place of one they had brought from London, and whom Lord Denton had never taken a fancy to. Helen was almost glad that this trial had befallen her friend, the difference it had made in her was so noticeable.

"Oh! Helen," exclaimed Kate, after a most weary day with her husband, "if I had only been like you in the smallest

degree, how different I should feel now. I
always knew you were infinitely better and
truer. I could admire, but not imitate you;
and now what is the result of all my boasted
indifference to good things?"

"Well, dear Kate, be thankful that you
have come to see and think differently even
now. Why you are quite young still; and
you know how prone we all are to wander
from the right path of duty. The world
you have lived in is a dreadfully difficult
one. How any one could manage to be
'in' it and not 'of' it, I cannot imagine."

"Ah! it is very sweet of you, Helen, to
make even that excuse. But I believe if you
knew all, which you do not, and never will,
you would despise me, and not love and
kiss me."

"Indeed, Kate, I should not. It would
be a poor proof of my being in the least
bit better than you, as you say I am.
Whatever I am, Kate, I owe it all to my

dear mother's training and example, and
to a country life with plenty to do."

"You may well say that, Helen. If I
had had a mother's loving care I might
have been less gay and frivolous, or else,
perhaps, I am by nature worse than most
girls in my sphere of life. I cannot tell.
I only know I am full of fears, and doubts,
and repinings."

"But that will wear off, Kate, by-and-by.
You are worried and are not getting your
complete night's rest now. I can quite understand all you feel, and am so sorry, dear. I
was only saying to mother to-day what a
pleasure I feel in seeing you so very much
more like what I would have had you years
ago if I could have had my will. But come
now, Kate, and have some dinner; then you
must really lie down on the sofa for the rest
of the evening till Dr. Andrews comes."

Dr. Andrews was not at all satisfied with
his Lordship's progress, and Lady Denton's

·quick eye detected this the moment she saw him after he had seen her husband. If there was no change for the better on the morrow, he said he should telegraph to London for a consultation with his brother practitioner, who had attended Lord Denton if ever he had required any one in London, to which, of course, Kate willingly consented. But the next day he was considerably better, and wished to be lifted from the bed to the sofa near the window.

It was a lovely, sunny afternoon; the autumn tints on the trees in the park were rich in their fading profusion and variety. The deer might have known that the master's eye was upon them, for they had all come down to the front of the house, and were walking lazily about on the smooth lawn. All was calm and quiet, and peacefully still. Kate sat near him, and had been reading aloud to him.

"Could you stop a little now, Kate? I

want to talk to you : I have something particular I wish to say to-day. I feel so much better—able, in fact, to tell you everything."

" Oh ! I can stop certainly," replied Kate, willing now to listen for any length of time if it would do him any good ; " but don't make any effort. I will come nearer ; there, I can hear you without you raising your voice."

She seated herself on a low stool nearer the head of the sofa, and put her hand on his, and waited for him to begin. He told her slowly what had been his secret, and what he had wanted to tell her on that evening in Paris after their marriage : how that three or four years before he first saw her he had, under most painful and extra-ordinary circumstances, met a young Swiss girl, about eighteen or nineteen, who had come over to England, as she thought, to a situation as nursery-governess to some young children ; but she had been cruelly and

shamefully deceived. Her appeal to him was
so heart-rending and pitiable, that he could
not leave her where she was. He took her
away with him at once, and placed her in
lodgings. He did not know what to do
after that. He knew no one to whose care
he could take her. She was innocent, and
pure, and good; so he married her. He
said nothing of this to any one until she
died, when he took Captain Martin into his
confidence.

He at first intended putting her in a
convent to improve her education, but she
fell into ill health, and when she gave birth
to her child—a boy—she died. He buried
her in the little country churchyard of the
place where she had gone for her health;
and an old Frenchwoman, who had come
over to nurse her, had the charge of the
baby till he was able to run about. Then
he had put him (in consequence of Annette's
ill-health) under the care of the wife of an

old friend, who, having no children of their own, took him as a favour, he being so young.

At the time of his marriage, he went on to say, the child was so ill that no one expected it to live, therefore he had said nothing about its existence. Then came to him news of his recovery, and he had determined to tell her everything; but something always happened to put him off, and he had gone on and on, keeping it from her, not knowing and scarcely thinking how it would end.

Although he had married the child's mother, he solemnly declared he had never loved her. Pity for her forlorn condition induced him to act as he did; but he had never until he met Kate truly and sincerely loved any woman.

He had one favour to ask of her now, and that was to send to Mr. Gresham immediately, and tell him to bring his boy to see

him once again. He asked this with as
much humility as if he had been in a prison
cell, and had no real right to expect so great
a favour.

How Kate sat still and listened, she
never could understand. She made no
attempt to stop her husband as he recalled
past events. The only movement was to
take her hand off his as he mentioned the
child's birth. What cruel fate had made
them both act with so little truth and
candour to each other? Had he only told
her this when she first knew him,—or at
least he most surely ought to have let her
father know,—how much more seriously
she would have thought of the step she
took when she became his wife.

She showed no sign of anger or resentment now to him. He and she were both
to blame, and nothing that they could either
say or do would alter the past. Thank
God that her baby had died! she said to

herself, it would have been a thousand times harder to bear than even this, to see him supplanted and second to the child of another woman, whose very existence had been unknown to her. She could not have borne that—it would have crushed her to the earth, and perhaps made her more wicked and sinful than she had already been.

She wrote her husband's wishes for the lad to come as soon as possible. He thanked her again and again for her forbearance. He knew, he said, he did not deserve it, and what a blow all this must be to her pride. But just then Kate wondered if she had even a touch of pride left; not that she wanted to call it to her aid in any way,—no, she felt humbled and grieved, and took the opportunity of saying how much she knew she was to blame for their cold, cheerless life.

"My dear Kate, God only knows what will be! I fear my days are few indeed now. I shall soon follow all that have gone before. I wish I could at least leave you with less regret. I am surely—"

"Oh, George, I entreat you to say no more now. You have talked so long, I am afraid you will do yourself harm. Try to rest, and we will talk again by-and-by."

Lady Denton was really alarmed. She was afraid his mind was going to ramble again, he looked so nervous and excited; but it was no use trying to quiet him. Having once begun, he could not confine himself to a few words; and when Dr. Andrews came later on in the day, he looked graver than ever, and prohibited so much talking going on in the sick-room.

Kate went to Miss Casteldi and told her all Lord Denton had said to her. There seemed to be no end of surprises and troubles for them. She did her best to console poor Kate after she realized what had come so suddenly to them. But how little one can do or say to make grief more bearable or

less keen, however well-intentioned one may
be!

"*What* shall I do, Aunt Neta, when that
boy comes? How degraded I feel to have
been kept in ignorance of his existence all
these years! How can I see and welcome
him? It is almost impossible, and yet I
want to do what is right and best, if I can.
How cruel Fate has been to me!"

"But, my darling Kitty, you must not
give way now. *He* cannot help, poor child!
being the unfortunate cause of your sorrow.
Take him freely, Kate, to your heart, and
let him fill the void you have so often regretted to me, and supply the place of his
poor dead mother so far as you can. Do
promise me that you will."

Kate did promise to try, although she
naturally could not help thinking of the
sensation it would cause, as every one would
know that she had been as ignorant about
the future heir as they had.

The next day a carriage from Denton
Court was sent to the station to fetch Mr.
Gresham and his young friend. He was
delicate-looking, and thin, not in the least
resembling the father who was impatiently
awaiting his coming. He had been told
how ill his father was, and that he was
going home. The word sounded strange
to the boy's ear, for he had never known
any home but the one they were taking him
from.

He knew really very little of his father,
although he had often seen him. He had
been told another lady filled his mother's
place, and he must wait till he was quite
grown up before he could see her, and not
ask questions. As he was not in the least
curious, and very obedient, he had gone
on, year after year, very happy where he
was, and not troubling his boyish mind a
bit about what he could not understand.

Kate met the lad with her aunt in the

·hall. It was an awkward moment for them all; but Mr. Gresham, although he had never seen her, knew her instantly, and said to the lad, "This is Lady Denton."

She told him all she could to prepare him for the alteration he would see in his father, and found, when she asked how long it was since he had seen him, that it was only a day or two before the accident.

"May I go to him now, please?" he said.

"Yes, almost directly, if you will try and be brave and quiet," Kate replied, kindly, seeing the effort he made to keep back his tears. "This lady, my aunt, will go with you," she added, as she smoothed his hair back which fell over his forehead.

"And you too, please," he said, taking her hand and drawing her with him. Her lovely face had taken his boyish fancy at once. She could not refuse the appeal of those two tearful eyes; and so they went in together, wife and child, so near to him who

lay there, and yet so far from each other in
actual relationship.

The boy made one bound on to his father's
bed; his arms were round him, his lips
quivering, and tears falling fast: he laid
his fair young face side by side of the
wasted one on the pillow, and entirely
forgot his promise to be quite quiet.

"Oh, papa, papa! I am so sorry. I didn't
think you were as ill as this, papa."

Lady Denton could not stay with them—
it almost made her sob aloud to see the sad
meeting; she went softly outside of the
room, unnoticed by either of them. What
else happened in that short interview no one
knew. Long afterwards the boy told Kate
that his father had made him promise always
to respect and love her, for his sake.

Lord Denton's presentiment about himself
proved true, for he lived only a few days
after his child came home. He died apparently without a struggle or pain.

His wife's and boy's names were the last distinct words he said, and they had to carry the latter away to his own bed, so overcome was he at the awful, still sight of his father's dead face.

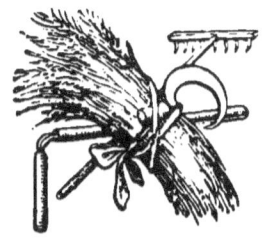

CHAPTER XI.

ADY DENTON heard them say he was gone, and yet she scarcely moved or noticed them as she stood near, with hot brow and cold hands, tearless, and almost vainly endeavouring to believe that it was verily and indeed true. Would he never breathe nor speak again to her? Was he gone away for ever, so gently and peacefully? Could *that* be death? Then, as she thought thus, she moved nearer, and felt the pale brow; and she knew that they were right, and allowed them to take her away.

"God bless and help you, darling," said Miss Casteldi, as she held her hands and bathed her forehead.

"Oh, Aunt Neta, this is so dreadful, so

hard to bear! It seems really dreadful to die and leave this world, however much we may have suffered in it!"

"Not, surely, my dear Kate, if we know and believe that we only exchange it for a brighter and better one of perfect rest and peace."

"Ah, if we know, aunt,—if we know! We cannot *know* what is before us; it is that which appals me so terribly."

"We need not try to know, Kate; we can leave all to One who has promised that to those who have faith, a place is prepared where no doubts nor fears nor change can come."

Kate closed her eyes and did not answer. She did not wish to distress her already sorrowing aunt by any more of her own complaints. Miss Casteldi was so much altered and considerably aged of late, that it was a grave matter of anxiety to her friends; and this last blow, coming so soon after the astonishing discovery of the heir, had been almost too much for her. Still, she soothed and cheered Kate as best she could, and scarcely ever complained of her own ailments.

Mr. Gresham's kind offer of help was gladly accepted by Lady Denton. There were no brothers on either side to get any assistance from, so that she was really pleased to have him stay till after the funeral. Mrs. Leigh had taken the boy to The Ridgway, Denton Court was such a sad home for him.

On the night of the day her husband died, when all the rest in the house had retired, Lady Denton took her candle, and went into the room where he lay, and turned the key in the door after her, to take a last look at the peaceful dead. She moved the white cloth from his face, and held the light above her head, so as to see the features more plainly. He was so like his former self, except for the marble whiteness; the face was, considering all he had gone through, very little changed. She placed her candle on a table near, and knelt down, clasping her hands, and prayed. Had any one been there, they would have heard no word nor whisper—no, not even a sigh nor a sob; but for the upturned face and moving lips, she too might have been lifeless.

What she prayed for, or what thoughts filled her soul, none can tell. In the gloomy stillness of that chamber, and in the presence of all that remained of him who ought to have been so dear to her, she may have imagined that his spirit was hovering round her, and that *he* knew what she said.

It was some time before she rose, and carefully replaced the covering after kissing the cold lips, and placing his hand across his chest, as she remembered to have seen her father lay. Those few solemn moments had done her good; she determined, with the aid of the help she had so earnestly prayed for, that she would give no more time nor thought to useless regret of the past, but live and work, and fill up what future came to her, and cast from her, as much as in her power lay, the selfish, delusive ideas and pleasures that had been so long her only object in life.

Of course Lord Denton's death caused a gloom over all their neighbourhood. He had always been so polite and hospitable whenever he had lived there, that he was thought to be a most good-hearted and easy-going acquaintance. Then his son's appearance was so astonishing; the most varied and absurd tales got afloat as to how and where he had come from. Very few knew anything really definitely true about him, but what they did not know they surmised, and positively believed.

Some pitied Lady Denton, as it was pretty certain she was not aware of anything of the

kind long before they were; others said,
who were not very well disposed or over-
charitable, that it served her right, and
would take down her pride an inch or
two.

Julia and Annie Clenning talked of nothing
else for days, and went purposely to Mrs.
Leigh's to glean a few stray scraps of reliable
information. Mrs. Leigh thought it best to
tell all she knew herself about it, and the
girls, as they rode home, wondered and con-
jectured how Lady Denton would go on after
the funeral, and if she would keep the boy
at home with her.

Poor Mrs. Clenning was terribly taken
aback. She at first refused to believe a word
of it; then her mind, usually so alive and
ready to catch at any unpleasant bit of news,
grasped the idea of it all, and took the
gloomiest possible view of its reality. How
ashamed she would be, she said, to see again
that poor deceived creature—meaning Lady

Denton. If she had not met him at her house, the remembrance of which had up till now been pleasant to her, she would not have minded half as much. Oh, the deceit of mankind in general, and noblemen in particular! Nothing, however base and vile, would surprise her now—no, not even the hearing that her own husband had hid away, somewhere in a remote corner of this nice little island of ours, another wife and family. Men were sad creatures, and so barefaced and insolent; no one should trust to anything they said.

This she told her husband when talking over what the girls had heard at Mrs. Leigh's; and Mr. Clenning assured her, solemnly and truly, that she need have no fear about there being a Mrs. Clenning number two, for he added, good-naturedly,—

"You and the girls have been almost too much for me to contend with from the beginning. I should have given up long ago if I had tried to double the burden."

When Bartle Blake heard of Lord Denton's death, he expressed a wish to follow him to the grave, and through Mrs. Leigh he heard that Lady Denton said "Yes." So he came over expressly for it from Dublin. It was a clear, bright day when the family vault in the pretty village church was opened to receive the remains of another member. The church was full of the tenantry, all in more or less mourning, and the friends and acquaintances of the neighbourhood.

To the surprise of many, Lady Denton came first with George, now Lord Denton, as chief mourners, who held her hand and kept close to her side, as the solemn service was read by the vicar. When the coffin was lowered, the poor child sobbed aloud, and many a tear of sympathy fell with his from others present. Every one was eager to get a good look at their future master, and some doubted, when they saw his delicate face, whether it would be long before the grave was opened again, so ill did he look, poor boy.

The will was short and concise; Lady Denton had an ample allowance left to her, and Mr. Gresham and a distant cousin of Lord Denton's were left the lad's guardians. If George could have had his way about future arrangements, the whole household from the Rectory would have taken up their abode at Denton; he said there was plenty of room for all the boys, and Mr. and Mrs. Gresham too. However, this was scarcely practicable; but Mr. Gresham kindly spared his assistant, whom George was very fond of, and who was a capital scholar, to come and reside at Denton, and continue the boy's studies till he went to College.

This was quite satisfactory; for although he had been so happy there, he very naturally preferred the freedom of a large country house and park, and the exclusive attention and companionship of his favourite tutor.

Lady Denton took great pains to have him taught to ride well. She often went out with him herself in the cold, sharp winter which followed his home-coming. He lost, in a great measure, the wan, sickly look he had had, and sometimes a colour would be seen in his cheeks, especially after any out-door game or exercise.

Nothing appeared to give him greater pleasure, either in or out of doors, than to be with her. He would come and sit with her sometimes, and tell her about his school-days, his illnesses, Mrs. Gresham (who, by the way, he wrote to every week regularly), his father's visits to him, what he used to say when he came, and the delightful toys that he brought; and once, soon after his things were sent home, he showed a small bundle of letters which his father had written to him and wanted Kate to read them.

Then there was old Annette to talk about, who used to come and see him sometimes; and when she was ill, his father took him to see her. He stayed a long time with her in her little cottage one day, and she told him all about his own mamma who had died there, Annette said, and she was buried in the churchyard not very far off. He asked his papa to take him to see her grave,—Annette told him he ought to see it; but his papa said they were late,—another day he should go; he did not go there again, or ever see Annette any more. But she told him, he said, all about his father's new wife, and said "you were very proud and cold,—a cruel mother," he added, " which I thought then was true. Of course poor old Annette did not know how very good you are, or I am sure she never would have said what she did about you."

"Good!" thought Lady Denton, as she listened to the lad's chatter. She had no claim to such a word: he little knew what pangs shot through her heart as he told her these things in his open, trusting fashion. She schooled herself to bear it, however, and returned his caresses, hoping he might never have cause to think her any less good than he did now. He called her "mother" so naturally from the first, that although the pleasure of hearing that sweetest of all names from the lips of any little one really belonging to her own self had been denied her, she could not attempt to prevent the child of him who had, she now believed, loved her so dearly, from calling her and loving her as a parent in whom he might place perfect trust and confidence.

As far as they could all judge, he was thoroughly truthful and straightforward, without the slightest tendency to equivocate or deceive, which was a great comfort to Lady Denton.

" When are we going to London, mother, to

see the sights? Papa often promised I should go, and stay ever so long. Couldn't we all go together this fine weather—Mr. Brett, and you, and auntie, and Norah? I am sure it would do us all good," he added confidently, thinking, perhaps, he could use no better reason for the necessity of his plan being carried out.

"I don't think I shall go to London this year, George; but I dare say, if you could manage without Norah and me, that you and Mr. Brett, and perhaps Aunt Neta, might be spared for a few weeks. Auntie wants to go to be near her dentist, and you would have to help look after her and see that she does not fatigue herself."

"It would be ever so much nicer if you went too, mother; but indeed I will take care of auntie, and I should so very much like to go, if you will let me."

So when spring had fairly set in, he was taken to town, and allowed to enjoy himself to his heart's content. She heard daily accounts of the youthful visitor's doings. He wrote scratchy, loving letters to her, full of all the fun he was having; and always ended with regrets for her absence, and how much he would have to tell her when he came home again.

Lady Denton had particularly requested Mr. Brett not to leave him alone with Captain Martin, if he should chance to call to see him or meet him anywhere. She had not altered her opinion of him in the least; on the contrary, she had seen letters which proved that he had had her husband completely in his power; therefore she determined that, as far as she could, she would prevent his seeing the boy, or gaining any influence over him. However, she was relieved to find that they had not come across him anywhere; and Miss Casteldi heard from some friends that he had wintered abroad, and had not yet returned to England.

While they were away, Kate did a good
deal of visiting among the poor. She and
Helen often met now in cottages where long
ago the latter could not even persuade her
to enter. Wasn't she a real lady?—a good
soul?—and didn't she speak to a poor body
so sweet like? were the common expressions
they used about her. She used sometimes
to pop in in the morning when Mrs. Andrews
was very busy, and sit for an hour or so
with the invalid sister. In fact, she did all
these things just as easily and with as much
tact as she entertained her wealthy guests.
She received every attention from her neighbouring friends. Not one word was ever
breathed or look shown before her to give
her an idea of the extreme curiosity which
had been felt, far and near, as to the late
events. They called to see her, and found
her subdued, and quiet, perhaps, for her, but
as dignified as ever.

She spoke of the boy as if she had known

. him all his life, and answered all their questions about how he was going on in town
with much apparent interest and pleasure.
It was not very long before the whole affair
ceased to be so very much talked about or
wondered at by her friends. He might have
been born and bred and lived every day of
his young life there, for the little notice that
was taken of him. It was quite natural to
see and hear of him at Denton; and he
might have been Kate's own child, so
thoroughly did the two seem to suit and
belong to each other as well as to the
house.

The strange discovery of an heir to the
Denton estate caused a good deal of talk and
gossip in the London circles. Every one
who knew her decided that Lady Denton
had been shamefully used by her husband.
Some blamed, some pitied her; and some of
her acquaintances wondered if she would
come to town that season, and take her usual

place as a handsome widow with a neat fortune, to make all the marrying men ready
to die of love for the privilege of court-
ing her smiles and favourable impressions.
Mrs. Gilbert went so far as to say she was
pretty sure she knew *who* the fortunate
individual was who would next claim Lady
Denton as a wife.

CHAPTER XII.

THIS story is drawing to a close. We have tried to show how a beautiful woman failed to find any contentment or happiness in marrying, for wealth and position, a man whom she did not love, and with whom she had no tastes or wishes in common. We have followed her through a few years of fashionable slavery and dissipation, until, by a merciful interposition of Providence, her plans for a last struggle for some peace and independence were frustrated, and she was led back to her wifely duty, and learned, late as it was, to look upon life as having wider and better things to do than wasting day after day, and year after year, in frivolous absurdities.

Helen and she became as close friends as ever, and many were the comforting truths she laid hold of from Mrs. Leigh's motherly advice and consolation. Helen Leigh had a new-found happiness to tell her friend, Mr. Blake having, before he returned to Ireland, asked her to gladden his future by becoming his wife. He confessed to her all his first love for Lady Denton,—all he had suffered in consequence of her refusing him. How he had, after a year or two, felt convinced that he had made a mistake in allowing himself to be so much with her, dazzled by her beauty and apparent preference for him; he knew then that she had never cared for him any more than for the rest of her friends.

"Heaven only knows the depth of the love I had for her then, Helen. I would have toiled and slaved for her willingly had it been necessary to do so; but as I came to think more soberly and less passionately, I knew it was all for the best; and if after this, Helen, you do not despise me, say 'Yes,' and make my future happier than I deserve."

They were in the garden where we first saw Helen, and Rover was there too, not quite as active and buoyant though. Perhaps he was impressed with the important subject under consideration, for when Helen and Bartle rose up to go into the house (after Helen had told him that she had loved him all her life; "at least," she added, blushing as much as ever, "since I first met you at Blackrock"), he went off before them at a sharp trot, wagging his tail, full of delight, although no notice had been taken of him by either his mistress or his future master.

Mrs. Leigh now understood why her daughter had been so disinclined to marry before. Of course she gave her consent to the engagement, hard as it was for her to look forward to losing Helen; but she did not say a word about it to them; for how could she be so selfish, when Helen had so long and so sacredly kept her secret, without allowing it to make the slightest difference to her or interfere with her love and duty to her mother?

Mr. Blake had to hurry back to his friends, who had gone to the West of Ireland. Then he had no chance of coming to The Ridgway as he passed through England on his way to Russia; but he intended to return for some time in a few months, when they were to have a quiet wedding in the village church.

Helen was almost ashamed of being so full of happiness while her friend Lady Denton was so sad and lonely, so she said nothing to her or any one else in the neighbourhood for a few weeks, till Kate had got over the worst and was more resigned. The Misses Clenning were very delighted when their mother told them, having had a visit from Mrs. Leigh, who had told her.

"I am glad," said Annie. "I had positively made up my mind to Helen never marrying, and living here all the days of her life. But 'better late than never,' Julia, as the old proverb tells us. It must be your turn next; and if I don't go off soon myself, I shall rush to some convent and beg to be taken in, as a creature weary of the world and its want of appreciation of my charms and recommendations."

Helen went that same day to Denton Court, and intended telling Kate her good news. As they were sitting chatting before the lights were brought in, she began her story. It was a strange coincidence that she should, some years before, have listened to the same thing from the woman she was now, in her turn, making a *confidante* of; and that the man whom Kate had so proudly rejected should have been the most dear in all the world to her.

Kate listened, and as Helen went on she was so thankful they had no light in the room. How her heart beat and her head throbbed! How could she wish her joy? Was it possible that Helen, so thoroughly unlike her in every respect and sense of the word, could fill the place she once held? Had he so entirely forgotten her and those happy days at home? Ah, well! why not? After all, her conduct had been such as to lead him to conclude that she had never cared a rush for him.

There was one thing pretty certain,—Helen had not guessed her secret, that she felt sure of; for she would not have said half so much to her if she had for a moment thought it would recall the past to her in any painful manner. So she got up and kissed Helen, and said all that was kind and womanly, and hoped she might be spared the trials and troubles that had fallen to her.

"Thanks, dear Kate. I don't expect to escape, I assure you. I only hope we may help each other to bear whatever comes; but it is early to anticipate coming evil. My only distress is, and I feel it very deeply, the idea of leaving my precious mother. She feels it too, I know, although, poor darling! she does not say much about it to me. I can't imagine how either of us will get on without the other, and scarcely dare mention it to her."

As the London season went on, and Lady Denton did not make her appearance at all, her friends were a good deal surprised. How she could live on there they could not understand; perhaps she had not got over her mortification, and could not show herself in consequence of that. Very few gave her credit for staying away from choice. She wished to make people curious and talk about

her, they said. Some went even so far as
to say, that perhaps she had found irresist-
ible attractions out of London, which kept
her at Denton; and every one declared she
would only remain a widow the bare time
society allows for proper mourning.

Captain Martin came back to London before the season was over. He, too, expected
to have found her Ladyship there. He
wondered how she had borne the boy coming home as heir to everything. And Mrs.
Gilbert detailed all the scraps of news she
had picked up here and there about her. She
still kept on her "nut-shell," as she called
her house; appeared as young and vigorous
as ever; still said spiteful things of the world
in general and her friends in particular;
still made hasty friendships, whenever she
got the chance to add a fresh addition to
her small, select circle, and managed somehow very cleverly to live in ease and plenty.

When Lady Denton did go to town, Mrs.

Gilbert found herself quietly and decidedly repulsed. Whatever influence or fascination there had been either in her or her choice friends, it was lost and gone for ever; so much so, that she did not attempt to pretend to any appearance of friendship with Kate. She assured every one who mentioned the difference they could but notice to her, that Lady Denton had turned saint, and, as she was such a sinner, it was impossible to feel at home with such an exalted being; so she wisely kept aloof, for fear of contaminating her.

Spring was fast giving place again to her next and, perhaps, more beautiful sister, Summer, when a small bridal party were assembled in a pretty village church, which was gaily decorated, and well filled with a neatly-dressed, anxious crowd of country people. Wives and mothers had got up earlier, and tidied up the cottages and children, and hastened there, determined to see Miss Helen wedded.

Bonny village children were there too; girls, away from the rest, under the guidance of some farmers' daughters, with baskets of lovely flowers, impatiently awaiting to be allowed to throw them before their dear Miss Helen. "Would she never come?" they asked again and again, every moment seeming ages to them.

The four bridesmaids—two of them we have seen before at the same kind of ceremony—were also waiting anxiously, for the bride was rather late. Mr. Blake was in the vestry, trying to appear as unconcerned as men usually do under such trying circumstances, but in reality as fluttered and nervous as a girl of sixteen (we could have said *boy*, but boys of that age are so seldom nervous),—moving restlessly about, and making spasmodic attempts at conversation with Mr. Clayton and the rest of his friends, and peeping out every now and then to see if Helen was coming.

At last the buzz ceased, the bridesmaids and guests arranged themselves on either side, and Mr. Benson, looking almost but not quite as cross as ever, walked down the aisle with the bride on his arm. He had said to her, as she came down to him,—

"Now, Helen, no fuss mind. I hate to see a woman crying at a wedding."

He was not, however, ill pleased to be present and give her away, but he never seemed able to *show* any satisfaction. Surely *his* face was not the index of his mind always, as some one somewhere says it is.

Mrs. Leigh was there, looking so dignified and bonny, Mr. and Mrs. Clenning, Dr. and Mrs. Andrews; in fact, all the neighbouring friends.

Lady Denton had come at the earnest desire of Helen. It had been a promise of long standing between them that, if possible, they should each be present at the other's wedding; and as Helen had fulfilled her part of the compact, Kate had to give way and be one of the number. She had. put off her deep mourning, and wore a grey silk, rich, and long, and full, with the usual soft lace and tulle about her wrists and neck.

How grand and noble she looked as she walked into the church with Lord Denton at her side! The people made way for her respectfully, and bowed and curtseyed as she passed, smiling and nodding in return to them.

But of course Helen Leigh, the fair little bride, was the observed of all observers to-day. They ranged themselves round the latter. Mr. Clayton began the service; but as Mr. Blake took the ring to place it on Helen's finger, he let it fall on the stone floor somewhere out of sight. Lady Denton saw it distinctly lying near a fold of her gown, but had her life depended on it she could not have stooped or even moved to pick it up; it would have scorched her

hand, she thought, had she touched it for
an instant. Sharp young eyes saw it too
almost directly after it fell, and the bridegroom received it again from Lord Denton.
This was only seen by those nearest. Some
of the guests did not know what had
happened to cause the slight commotion,
it was so soon over.

If Lady Denton could have believed at
that moment that any ill would befall those
two beings whom that tiny circlet had made
one for ever, her superstitious tendency to
put faith in signs would have suggested that
the falling of the ring was a bad one. She
took leave of the bride and her husband in
the vestry after the signing of the register.
Miss Casteldi and George were going on
to The Ridgway for the breakfast.

She stayed there till all the company had
left the church, and then she drove home,
where she was alone for some hours. How
she wept that afternoon, and thought of

what might have been, if— Ah! if—only
if! What a tiny word, and yet how often
we use it when it expresses such volumes
of doubt, or fear, or regret, or hope!

We can scarcely wonder at or blame Lady
Denton indulging and thinking of how different her life might have been. If she
was wrong, surely those tears would blot
out her sin. Any one would have pitied
her as she sat in her room, holding her
forehead, which was throbbing painfully,
and drying her eyes, repeating inwardly,
"Gone for ever, for ever!"

That she had loved Bartle Blake from the
very first as only women like her can love,
there is not a shadow of a doubt; and to
stand by and see him take another woman
to his heart and home, must have been a
severe punishment for her girlish pride and
wilfulness.

Miss Casteldi, when she returned, told
Kate all about the breakfast, &c. Of course

Mrs. Leigh felt Helen's leaving very much. Mr. Benson kept protesting against the absurdity of scenes of all kinds, although Miss Casteldi added he looked as inclined to cry as any one.

This must have been a pure fabrication of her aunt's fancy. Such a grumpy old gentleman as Mr. Benson could not have even had a desire to do anything so beneath his dignity, we think.

The happy pair started for the Continent before Miss Casteldi left, and she said that Helen looked so beamingly full of bright anticipation of returning, and bore up wonderfully when they went away. Things had been arranged much to Helen's and her mother's satisfaction.

Mr. Blake intended to settle in England, although the getting away from his present post was no easy matter, he found. His employers had thought him so clever and reliable, that they were loth to part with him, and offered an increase of salary for him to stay there. But there was an opening for him at home, and with his prosperity he had not, mercifully, learned to look upon money as the greatest thing in this world to live for, so he decided to remain in England, and finally bade adieu to Russia and the kind friends he had there.

But it was not the last he saw of his friend Mr. Nitikin, for he came to pay a visit to them at The Ridgway some years after: when little feet toddled about in the house and garden, and little tongues prattled there too, and made the old house bright and joyous; when Mrs. Leigh's hair was quite white, her hands and head trembling, but her face smiling and contented, as she sits knitting in her easy-chair, listening to all the sounds from merry voices, while Rover, a petted favourite still, though nearly blind, lies enjoying the warm sun, by the side of his now no longer youthful mistress, and

Bartle Blake, more prosperous than ever,
declares he is the most fortunate fellow in
all the world.

Lord Denton has grown a tolerably
fine man, rather taller than his father,
and not nearly so stout. He fairly
distinguished himself at College, and is
now at Denton Court, making a short stay
previous to starting for a tour on the Continent.

Mr. Brett had, through some assistance
from Lady Denton, opened a good school for
boys when he left Denton; and so much had
she exerted herself to get him pupils, that
he had done wonderfully well. George had
just returned from a visit to him on his way
home, and told his mother "that Mr. Brett
was looking fat and flourishing."

"All through your kindness, mother. He
talks of you with such sincere respect and
admiration, there is no mistaking how he
values your friendship and help. You are

his good angel, he says, and of course I agree with him."

Such words as these must surely have made Kate feel that she was now useful to others, and employing better the precious time and talents that had been entrusted to her. She went with the young man to London, where he was to meet the gentleman who was to accompany him and three other young men on their travels. She had taken great pains to secure a pleasant, educated companion for him, and had every reason to think she had been most successful in her choice.

So she saw them fairly started on their journey one early summer morning. As they were taking leave, he said, placing his arm around her affectionately,—

" Couldn't you come too, mother, even now."

" Decidedly not, you selfish boy. What would become of Aunt Neta if I did ?"

"Ah, what indeed, mother. She would be lonely without you. I forgot her for the moment. Good-bye, God bless you! Take a kiss for auntie, and don't tell her I suggested taking you away from her."

"Good-bye, George; be sure you write often, and tell me all about everything."

Lady Denton never married again, in spite of the arrangements her friends had made about her doing so. She lived most of her time at Denton Court, devoted to her aunt, who lived much longer than any one could have supposed she would from the delicate state of her health of late years.

Lord Denton came in for the Dukedom, and married a fair, blue-eyed gentle girl, whom Lady Denton loved very much, and whose children were petted and, perhaps, spoiled by their beautiful, stately Grand-mamma Denton, as they called her.

THE END.

LONDON: PRINTED BY
EDWARD J. FRANCIS, TOOK'S COURT,
CHANCERY LANE, E.C.

SAMUEL TINSLEY'S

PUBLICATIONS.

London:

SAMUEL TINSLEY,

10, SOUTHAMPTON STREET, STRAND.

. *Totally distinct from any other firm of Publishers.*

16

NOTICE.

The PRINTING and PUBLICATION of all Classes of BOOKS, Pamphlets, &c.— Apply to MR. SAMUEL TINSLEY, *Publisher,* 10, *Southampton Street, Strand, London, W.C.*

BETWEEN TWO LOVES. By ROBERT J. GRIF-
FITHS, LL.D.   3 vols., 31s. 6d.

BORN TO BE A LADY. By KATHERINE HEN-
DERSON.   Crown 8vo., 7s. 6d.

"Miss Henderson has written a really interesting story. . . . The heroine,
Jeanie Monroe, is just what a Jeanie should be—'bonny,' 'sonsie,' 'douce,'
and 'eident,'—having a fair and sound mind in a fair and sound body ;
loving and loyal, true to earthly love, and firm to heavenly faith. The
novelist's art is exhibited by marrying this gardener's daughter to a man
of shifting principles, higher in a sense than she in the social scale. . . .
The 'local colouring' is excellent, and the subordinate characters, Jeanie's
father especially, capital studies."—*Athenæum.*

BUILDING UPON SAND. By ELIZABETH J.
LYSAGHT.   Crown 8vo., 10s. 6d.

" It is an eminently lady-like story, and pleasantly told. . . . . We
can safely recommend 'Building upon Sand.'"—*Graphic.*

CHASTE AS ICE, PURE AS SNOW. By Mrs.
M. C. DESPARD.   3 vols., 31s. 6d.   Second Edition.

" A novel of something more than ordinary promise."—*Graphic.*

CRUEL CONSTANCY. By KATHARINE KING,
Author of 'The Queen of the Regiment.'   3 vols., 31s. 6d.

" It is a very readable novel, and contains much pleasant writing." —*Pall
Mall Gazette.*

" In this story Miss King has made an advance. She has avoided many
of the faults which are so apparent in ' Lost for Gold,' and she has bestowed
much pains upon delineation of character and descriptions of Irish life.
Her book possesses originality."—*Morning Post.*

DISINTERRED.   From the Boke of a Monk of
Carden Abbey.   By T. ESMONDE.   Crown 8vo., 7s. 6d.

DR. MIDDLETON'S DAUGHTER. By the Author
of " A Desperate Character."   3 vols., 31s. 6d.

FAIR, BUT NOT WISE. By Mrs. FORREST-GRANT.
2 vols., 21s.

" ' Fair but not Wise ' possesses considerable merit, and is both cleverly
and powerfully written. If earnest, it is yet amusing and sometimes
humorous, and the interest is well sustained from the first to the last
page."—*Court Express.*

FIRST AND LAST. By F. VERNON-WHITE. 2 vols.,
21s.

FLORENCE; or, Loyal Quand Même. By FRANCES
ARMSTRONG. Crown 8vo., 5s., cloth. Post free.

" It is impossible not be interested in the story from beginning to end."
—*Examiner.*

"A very charming love story, eminently pure and lady-like in tone,
effective and interesting in plot, and, rarest praise of all, written in excellent
English."—*Civil Service Review.*

" The book is excellently printed and nicely bound- in fact it is one
which authoress, publisher, and reader may alike regard with mingled
satisfaction and pleasure."—*Nottingham Daily Guardian.*

" ' Florence ' is readable, even interesting in every part."—*The Scotsman.*

FOLLATON PRIORY. 2 vols., 21s.

" 'Follaton Priory' is a thoroughly sensational story, written with
more art than is usual in compositions of its class ; and avoiding, skilfully,
a melancholy termination."—*Sunday Times.*

GAUNT ABBEY. By ELIZABETH J. LYSAGHT, Author of
" Building upon Sand," " Nearer and Dearer," etc. 3 vols.,
31s. 6d.

GOLDEN MEMORIES. By EFFIE LEIGH. 2 vols.,
21s.

" There is not a dull page in the book." *–Morning Post.*

GRAYWORTH: a Story of Country Life. By CAREY
HAZELWOOD. 3 vols., 31s. 6d.

" Carey Hazelwood can write well."—*Examiner.*

" Many traces of good feeling and good taste, little touches of quiet
humour, denoting kindly observation, and a genuine love of the country."—
Standard.

HER GOOD NAME. By J. FORTREY BOUVERIE.
3 vols., 31s. 6d.

" Who steals my purse steals trash : 'Tis something, nothing ;
'Twas mine, 'tis his, and has been slave to thousands ;
But he that filches from me my good name
Robs me of that, which not enriches him,
And makes me poor indeed."

Othello.

HILDA AND I. By MRS. WINCHCOMBE HARTLEY.
2 vols., 21s.

HILLESDEN ON THE MOORS. By Rosa Mackenzie Kettle, Author of "The Mistress of Langdale
Hall." 2 vols., 21s.

"Thoroughly enjoyable, full of pleasant thoughts gracefully expressed,
and eminently pure in tone."—*Public Opinion.*

IN SECRET PLACES. By Robert J. Griffiths,
LL.D. 3 vols., 31s. 6d.

IS IT FOR EVER? By Kate Mainwaring. 3 vols.,
31s. 6d.

"A work to be recommended. . . . . A thrillingly sensational novel."—
Sunday Times.

JOHN FENN'S WIFE. By Maria Lewis.
Crown 8vo., 7s. 6d.

KATE BYRNE. By S. Howard Taylor. 2 vols.,
21s.

KITTY'S RIVAL. By Sydney Mostyn, Author of
'The Surgeon's Secret,' etc. 3 vols., 31s. 6d.

"Essentially dramatic and absorbing. . . . . We have nothing but
unqualified praise for 'Kitty's Rival,' which we recommend as a fresh and
natural story, full of homely pathos and kindly humour, and written in a
style which shows the good sense of the author has been cultivated by the
study of the works of the best of English writers."—*Public Opinion.*

LORD CASTLETON'S WARD. By Mrs. B. R.
Green. 3 vols., 31s. 6d.

"This is novel of character as well as of incident, and Mrs. Green has
been studious in balancing fairly the two elements which combine to make
her work not only interesting but instructive. The events are pleasingly
described, and are of a nature to arrest attention. They are natural and
dramatic, and so arranged as to succeed each other with increasing interest.
The plot, without being intricate, is sufficiently involved to create a desire
to follow its development and conclusion. . . . Mrs. Green has written a
readable story, fresh and bright. . . . It is very readable."—*Public Opinion.*

"There is a great deal of love-making in the book, an element which
will no doubt favourably recommend it to the notice of young lady
readers. . . . Being a novel suited to the popular taste, it is likely to
become a favourite. . . . Sensationalism is evidently aimed at, and here
the author has succeeded admirably. . . . Mrs. Green has written a novel
which will hold the reader entranced from the first page to the last. . . .
Emphatically a sensational novel of no ordinary merit, with plenty of stirring incident well and vividly worked out. . . . Florence de Malcé, the
heroine and Lord Castleton's ward, is a masterpiece."—*Morning Post.*

$\mathbf{M}$ARY GRAINGER: A Story. By George Leigh.
2 vols., 21s.

"A very remarkable, a wholly exceptional book. It is original from beginning to end ; it is full of indubitable power ; the characters, if they are such as we are not accustomed to meet with in ordinary novels, are nevertheless wonderfully real, and the reader is able to recognise the force and truth of the author's conceptions. The heroine is such a creation as would be looked for in vain in literature outside the pages of Balzac or George Sand—a noble but undeveloped character, of whom, nevertheless, we are inclined to believe that many a counterpart is to be found in real life."—*Scotsman.*

$\mathbf{M}$R. VAUGHAN'S HEIR. By Frank Lee Benedict, Author of "Miss Dorothy's Charge," etc. 3 vols., 31s. 6d.

$\mathbf{N}$EARER AND DEARER. By Elizabeth J. Lysaght, Author of "Building upon Sand." 3 vols., 31s. 6d.

"A capital story. . . very pleasant reading . . . With the exception of George Eliot, there is no other of our lady writers with whom Mrs. Lysaght will not favourably compare."—*Scotsman.*
"We have said the book is readable. It is more, it is both clever and interesting."—*Sunday Times.*

$\mathbf{N}$EGLECTED ; a Story of Nursery Education Forty Years Ago. By Miss Julia Luard. Crown 8vo., 5s. cloth.

$\mathbf{N}$OT TO BE BROKEN. By W. A. Chandler. Crown 8vo., 10s. 6d.

$\mathbf{O}$NLY SEA AND SKY. By Elizabeth Hindley. 2 vols., 21s.

$\mathbf{O}$VER THE FURZE. By Rosa M. Kettle, Author of the "Mistress of Langdale Hall," etc. 3 vols., 31s. 6d.

$\mathbf{N}$O FATHERLAND. By Madame Von Oppen. 2 vols., 21s.

$\mathbf{P}$ERCY LOCKHART. By F. W. Baxter. 2 vols., 21s.

"A bright, fresh, healthy story. . . . . Eminently readable."—*Standard.*
"The novel altogether deserves praise. It is healthy in tone, interesting in plot and incident, and generally so well written that few persons would be able justly to find fault with it."—*Scotsman.*

RAVENSDALE.   By Robert Thynne, Author of
"Tom Delany."   3 vols., 31s. 6d.
"A well-told, natural, and wholesome story."—*Standard*.
"No one can deny merit to the writer."—*Saturday Review*.

RUPERT REDMOND: A Tale of England, Ireland,
and America.   By Walter Sims Southwell.   3 vols.,
31s. 6d.

SHINGLEBOROUGH SOCIETY.   3 vols., 31s. 6d.

SONS OF DIVES.   2 vols., 21s.
"A well-principled and natural story."—*Athenæuri.*

STRANDED, BUT NOT LOST.   By Dorothy
Bromyard.   3 vols., 31s. 6d.

THE ADVENTURES OF MICK CALLIGHIN, M.P.
a Story of Home Rule ; and THE DE BURGHOS, a
Romance.   By W. R. Ancketill.   In one Volume, with Illustrations.   Price 7s. 6d.

THE BARONET'S CROSS.   By Mary Meeke,
Author of "Marion's Path through Shadow to Sunshine."
2 vols., 21s.
"A novel suited to the palates of eager consumers of fiction."—*Sunday
Times.*

THE D'EYNCOURTS OF FAIRLEIGH.   By
Thomas Rowland Skemp.   3 vols., 31s. 6d.
"An exceedingly readable novel, full of various and sustained interest.
. . . . The interest is well kept up all through."—*Daily Telegraph.*

THE HEIR OF REDDESMONT.   3 vols., 31s. 6d.
"Full of interest and life."—*Echo.*

THE INSIDIOUS THIEF: a Tale for Humble
Folks.   By One of Themselves.   Crown 8vo., 5s.   Second
Edition.

THE LOVE THAT LIVED.   By Mrs. Eiloart, Author
of "The Curate's Discipline," "Just a Woman," "Woman's
Wrong," &c.   3 vols., 31s. 6d.
"Three volumes which most people will prefer not to leave till they have
read the last page of the third volume."—*Pall Mall Gazette.*

"One of the most thoroughly wholesome novels we have read for some time."—*Scotsman.*

THE MAGIC OF LOVE. By Mrs. FORREST-GRANT, Author of "Fair, but not Wise." 3 vols., 31s. 6d.

"A very amusing novel."—*Scotsman.*
"Mrs. Forrest-Grant gives us a really original tale, the plot of which is alike well conceived and executed ; and the characters in which, whether good or bad, attract or repel the reader with resistless fascination. . . . It is a capital tale."—*John Bull.*

THE SECRET OF TWO HOUSES. By FANNY FISHER. 2 vols., 21s.

"Thoroughly dramatic."—*Public Opinion.*
"The story is well told."—*Sunday Times.*

THE SEDGEBOROUGH WORLD. By A. FARE-BROTHER. 2 vols., 21s.

"There is no little novelty and a large fund of amusement in 'The Sedgeborough World.'"—*Illustrated London News.*

THE SURGEON'S SECRET. By SYDNEY MOSTYN, Author of "Kitty's Rival," etc. Crown 8vo., 10s. 6d.

"A most exciting novel—the best on our list. It may be fairly recom-mended as a very extraordinary book."—*John Bull.*
"A stirring drama, with a number of closely connected scenes, in which there are not a few legitimately sensational situations. There are many spirited passages."--*Public Opinion.*

THE THORNTONS OF THORNBURY. By Mrs. HENRY LOWTHER CHERMSIDE. 3 vols., 31s. 6d.

THE TRUE STORY OF HUGH NOBLE'S FLIGHT. By the Authoress of "What Her Face Said." 10s. 6d.

"A pleasant story, with touches of exquisite pathos, well told by one who is master of an excellent and sprightly style."—*Standard.*
"An unpretending, yet very pathetic story. . . . We can congratu-late the author on having achieved a signal success."—*Graphic.*

TIMOTHY CRIPPLE ; or, "Life's a Feast." By THOMAS AURIOL ROBINSON. 2 vols., 21s.

"This is a most amusing book, and the author deserves great credit for the novelty of his design, and the quaint humour with which it is worked out."—*Public Opinion.*
"For abundance of humour, variety of incident, and idiomatic vigour of expression, Mr. Robinson deserves, and will no doubt receive, great credit."—*Civil Service Review.*

TOO LIGHTLY BROKEN. 3 vols., 31s. 6d.

"A very pleasing story . . . . . very prettily told."--*Morning Post.*

TOM DELANY. By ROBERT THYNNE, Author of "Ravensdale." 3 vols., 31s. 6d.

"A very bright, healthy, simply-told story."—*Standard.*

"All the individuals whom the reader meets at the gold-fields are well-drawn, amongst whom not the least interesting is 'Terrible Mac.'"—*Hour.*

"There is not a dull page in the book."—*Scotsman.*

TOWER HALLOWDEANE. 2 vols., 21s.

TWIXT CUP and LIP. By MARY LOVETT-CAMERON. 3 vols., 31s. 6d.

"Displays signs of more than ordinary promise. . . . As a whole the novel cannot fail to please. Its plot is one that will arrest attention; and its characters, one and all, are full of life and have that nameless charm which at once attracts and retains the sympathy of the reader."—*Daily News.*

WAGES: a Story in Three Books. 3 vols., 31s. 6d.

"A work of no commonplace character."— *Sunday Times.*

WANDERING FIRES. By Mrs. M. C. DESPARD, Author of "Chaste as Ice," &c. 3 vols., 31s. 6d.

WEBS OF LOVE. (I. A Lawyer's Device. II. Sancta Simplicitas.) By G. E. H. 1 vol., Crown 8vo., 10s. 6d.

WEIMAR'S TRUST. By Mrs. EDWARD CHRISTIAN. 3 vols., 31s. 6d.

"A novel which deserves to be read, and which, once begun, will not be readily laid aside till the end."—*Scotsman.*

WILL SHE BEAR IT? A Tale of the Weald. 3 vols., 31s. 6d.

"This is a clever story, easily and naturally told, and the reader's interest sustained throughout. . . . A pleasant, readable book, such as we can heartily recommend as likely to do good service in the dull and foggy days before us."—*Spectator.*

"Written with simplicity, good feeling, and good sense, and marked throughout by a high moral tone, which is all the more powerful from never being obtrusive. . . . The interest is kept up with increasing power to the last."—*Standard.*

NOTICE.—Miss Rosa M. Kettle's New Story.

OVER THE FURZE. By Rosa Mackenzie Kettle.
3 vols., 31s. 6d.

(From the PALL MALL GAZETTE, June 13th, 1874.)

This pleasantly-written story will be read with enjoyment by many people, especially young people, who are sure to admire the hero. He is, as Thackeray says of Scott's heroes, "handsome, brave, amiable, and not too clever," just the sort of person to charm a very young girl. Other characters in the book have, however, far more distinctness and life than Victor O'Ruark. The authoress has laid her story in the end of the last century, making the French attacks on Ireland the turning events of the book, and introducing us to a group of French refugees, Louis XVIII. among them, and of enthusiastic Irish patriots of good family and gentle manners. There is plenty of stirring incident in the story, which is decidedly above the average ; and the way in which it is introduced and told by the nun, who remembers it as connected with her own childhood, is most happy. Mdme. de Luneville, the intriguing Canoness de Rémiremont, is very well sketched, and old Ralph Durham, the gamekeeper, with his bright young wife, stands very clearly before us. But the best sustained character in the book, to our mind, is Lady Mostyn, of old Irish family. The independence of Ireland is the passion of her life, the object for which she economizes, and to which she willingly devotes even the nephew whom she loves best in the world. For her daughter she cares little, save as a possible bride for her beloved nephew, who is to lead the Irish rising in Connemara. A paralytic attack, brought on by anxiety, spares her a part of the pain of his defeat and banishment. Her daughter's devoted nursing softens her by degrees, and she lives to see the marriage which she had long desired. Irish patriotism in those days meant something very different from Fenianism. The old Catholic families were so closely connected with the French Court as to have gained much of its polish ; and the stirring events of this half-historical novel are graced by a pleasant setting of rustling silks and old china, and the courtly manners of the *émigrés* of the *ancien régime*.

(From the SCOTSMAN, June 19th, 1874.)

As a piece of literary workmanship, "Over the Furze" must be ranked higher than any of Miss Kettle's previous efforts; and in a time when clever writers of fiction are numerous, and when a book must possess exceptional merit to be remarkable, it is entitled to recognition as a novel of undoubted originality and considerable excellence. . . . The book is, on the whole, one which contains much genuinely good work, and will materially add to the author's reputation.

Samuel Tinsley, 10, Southampton Street, Strand.

Notice:

NEW SYSTEM OF PUBLISHING ORIGINAL NOVELS.

Vol. I.

THE MISTRESS OF LANGDALE HALL: a Romance of the West Riding. By ROSA MACKENZIE KETTLE. Complete in one handsome volume, with Frontispiece and Vignette by PERCIVAL SKELTON. 4s., post free.

(From THE SATURDAY REVIEW.)

Generally speaking, in criticising a novel we confine our observations to the merits of the author. In this case we must make an exception, and say something as to the publisher. The *Mistress of Langdale Hall* does not come before us in the stereotyped three-volume shape, with rambling type, ample margins, and nominally a guinea and a half to pay. On the contrary, this new aspirant to public admiration appears in the modest guise of a single graceful volume, and we confess that we are disposed to give a kindly welcome to the author, because we may flatter ourselves that she is in some measure a *protégée* of our own. A few weeks ago an article appeared in our columns censuring the prevailing fashion of publishing novels at nominal and fancy prices. Necessarily, we dealt a good deal in commonplaces, the absurdity of the fashion being so obvious. We explained, what is well known to every one interested in the matter, that the regulation price is purely illusory. The publisher in reality has to drive his own bargain with the libraries, who naturally beat him down. The author suffers, the trade suffers, and the libraries do not gain. Arguing that a palpable absurdity must be exploded some day unless all the world is qualified for Bedlam, we felt ourselves on tolerably safe ground when we ventured to predict an approaching revolution. Judging from the preface to this book, we may conjecture that it was partly on our hint that Mr. Tinsley has published. As all prophets must welcome events that tend to the speedy accomplishment of their predictions, we confess ourselves gratified by the promptitude with which Mr. Tinsley has acted, and we heartily wish his venture success. He recognises that a reformation so radical must be a work of time, and at first may possibly seem to defeat its object. For it is plain that the public must first be converted to a proper regard for its own interest ; and, by changing the borrowing for the buying system, must come in to buy the publisher out. He must look, moreover, to the support and imitation of his brethren of the trade. We doubt not he has made the venture after all due deliberation, and that we may rely on his determination seconding his enterprise. All prospectuses of new undertakings tend naturally to exaggeration, but success will be well worth the waiting for, should it be only the shadow of that on which Mr. Tinsley reckons. He gives some surprising figures ; he states some startling facts ; and, as a practical man, he draws some practical conclusions. He quotes a statement of Mr. Charles Reade's, to the effect that three publishers in the United States had disposed of no less than 370,000 copies of Mr. Reade's latest novel. He estimates that the profits on that sale—the book being published at a dollar—must amount to £25,000. Mr. Reade, of course, has a name, and we can conceive that his faults and blemishes may positively recommend themselves to American taste. But Mr. Tinsley remarks that if a publisher could sell 70,000 copies in any case, there would still be £5,000 of clear gain; and even if the new system had a much more moderate success than that, all parties would still profit amazingly. For Mr. Tinsley calculates the profits of a sale of 2,000 copies of a three volume edition at £1,000; and we should fancy the experience of most authors would lead them to believe he overstates it. It will be seen that at all events the new speculation promises brilliantly, and reason and common-sense conspire to tell us that the reward must come to him who has patience to wait. *Palmam qui meruit ferat*, and may he have his share of the profits too. Meanwhile, here we have the first volume of Mr. Tinsley's new series in most legible type, in portable form, and with a sufficiently attractive exterior. The price is four shillings, and, the customary trade deduction being made to circulating libraries, it leaves them without excuse should they deny it to the order of their customers.

The story is interesting and very pleasantly written, and for the sake of both author and publisher we cordially wish it the reception it deserves.

VOL. II.

PUTTYPUT'S PROTÉGÉE; or, Road, Rail, and River. A Story in Three Books. By HENRY GEORGE CHURCHILL. Crown 8vo., (uniform with "The Mistress of Langdale Hall"), with 14 illustrations by WALLIS MACKAY. Post free, 4s. Second edition.

"It is a lengthened and diversified farce, full of screaming fun and comic delineation—a reflection of Dickens, Mrs. Malaprop, and Mr. Boucicault, and dealing with various descriptions of social life. We have read and laughed, pooh-poohed, and read again, ashamed of our interest, but our interest has been too strong for our shame. Readers may do worse than surrender themselves to its melo-dramatic enjoyment. From title-page to colophon, only Dominie Sampson's epithet can describe it— it is ' prodigious.'"—*British Quarterly Review*.

"It is impossible to read ' Puttyput's Protégée ' without being reminded at every turn of the contemporary stage, and the impression it leaves on the mind is very similar to that produced by witnessing a whole evening's entertainment at one of our popular theatres."—*Echo*.

EPITAPHIANA; or, the Curiosities of Churchyard Literature : being a Miscellaneous Collection of Epitaphs, with an INTRODUCTION. By W. FAIRLEY. Crown 8vo., cloth, price 5s. Post free.

"Entertaining."—*Pall Mall Gazette.*
"A capital collection."—*Court Circular.*
"A very readable volume."—*Daily Review.*
"A most interesting book."—*Leeds Mercury.*
"Interesting and amusing."—*Nonconformist.*
"Particularly entertaining."—*Public Opinion.*
"A curious and entertaining volume."—*Oxford Chronicle.*
"A very interesting collection."—*Civil Service Gazette.*
"Although we have picked several plums from Mr. Fairley's book, we can assure our readers that there are plenty more left. And now that the long evenings are once more stealing upon us, and the fireside begins to be comfortable, suggesting a book and a quiet read, let us recommend Mr. Fairley, who comes before us in the handsome guise and the capital type of the enterprising Mr. Samuel Tinsley."—*Derbyshire Advertiser.*

HARRY'S BIG BOOTS : a Fairy Tale, for "Smalle Folke." By S. E. GAY. With 8 Full-page Illustrations and a Vignette by the author, drawn on wood by PERCIVAL SKELTON. Crown 8vo., handsomely bound in cloth, price 5s.

"'Harry's Big Boots' is sure of a large and appreciative audience. It is as good as a Christmas pantomime, and its illustrations are quite equal to any transformation scene. . . . The pictures of Harry and Harry's seven-leagued boots, with their little wings and funny faces, leave nothing to be desired."—*Daily News.*
"Some capital fun will be found in 'Harry's Big Boots.'. . . The illustrations are excellent, and so is the story."—*Pall Mall Gazette.*

MOVING EARS. By the Ven. Archdeacon WEAKHEAD, Rector of Newtown, Kent. 1 vol., crown 8vo., 5s.

A TRUE FLEMISH STORY. By the Author of "The Eve of St. Nicholas." In wrapper, 1s.

THE PHYSIOLOGY OF THE SECTS. Crown 8vo., price 5s.

ANOTHER WORLD; or, Fragments from the Star City of Montalluyah. By HERMES. Third Edition, revised, with additions. Post 8vo., price 12s.

THE FALL OF MAN : An Answer to Mr. Darwin's "Descent of Man ;" being a Complete Refutation, by common-sense arguments, of the Theory of Natural Selection. 1s., sewed.

Samuel Tinsley, 10, Southampton Street, Strand.

POETRY, Etc.

MISPLACED LOVE. A Tale of Love, Sin, Sorrow, and Remorse. 1 vol., crown 8vo., 5s.

THE SOUL SPEAKS, and other Poems. By FRANCIS H. HEMERY. In wrapper, 1s.

SUMMER SHADE AND WINTER SUNSHINE : Poems. By ROSA MACKENZIE KETTLE, Author of " The Mistress of Langdale Hall." New Edition. 2s. 6d., cloth.

THE WITCH of NEMI, and other Poems. By EDWARD BRENNAN. Crown 8vo., 10s. 6d.

MARY DESMOND, AND OTHER POEMS. By NICHOLAS J. GANNON. Fcp. 8vo., 4s., cloth. Second Edition.

THE GOLDEN PATH : a Poem. By ISABELLA STUART. 6d., sewed.

THE REDBREAST OF CANTERBURY CATHE- DRAL : Lines from the Latin of Peter du Moulin, some- time a Prebendary of Canterbury. Translated by the Rev. F. B. WELLS, M.A., Rector of Woodchurch. Handsomely bound, price 1s.

THE TICHBORNE AND ORTON AUTOGRAPHS; comprising Autograph Letters of Roger Tichborne, Arthur Orton (to Mary Ann Loder), and the Defendant (early letters to Lady Tichborne, &c.), in facsimile. In wrapper, price 6d.

BALAK AND BALAAM IN EUROPEAN COS- TUME. By the Rev. JAMES KEAN, M.A., Assistant to the Incumbent of Markinch, Fife. 6d., sewed.

ANOTHER ROW AT DAME EUROPA'S SCHOOL. Showing how John's Cook made an IRISH STEW, and what came of it. 6d., sewed.

NOTICE.—A new work by the Hon. Grantley F. Berkeley.

FACT AGAINST FICTION. The Habits and

Treatment of Animals Practically Considered.   Hydrophobia and Distemper.   With some remarks on Darwin.   By the HON. GRANTLEY F. BERKELEY.   2 vols., 8vo., 30s.

" It is refreshing to meet with a book like Mr. Berkeley's, written not only by a sportsman, but by a sportsman of the old school.........Taking his volumes all in all, they are an agreeable and useful contribution to a subject which he has studied with all his heart and soul through a long and active lifetime."—*Pall Mall Gazette.*

" Mr. Berkeley has lived with animals all his life, and has a happy knack of making friends with them.   Nor can we wonder at it when we see how keenly he loves them, how thoroughly he has come to understand their natures, and how closely he studies their individual characters and humours, their little weaknesses... .....Mr. Berkeley's hints on breeding and hunting hounds, on rearing and preserving game, are well worth reading ; but naturally it is not easy to do them justice in a brief notice.   In his talk about hounds, what strikes us is the close attention he has evidently paid to their habits, which makes his advice the more valuable.........But we may have said enough to show that the book is profitable as well as amusing."—*Saturday Review.*

" The godson of George the Fourth gives us here two rattling volumes, brimming with egotism, dogmatism, and aggressiveness, all to be forgiven, perhaps, because their author is a veteran, possessing real mastership of his subject, and one who writes from long and diversified experience.   All relating to hounds, foxes, horses, birds, wild fowl, fishes, game preserving, and poaching, comes by turn under his hand, and he never flinches from pronouncing an opinion.........Full of dash and sparkle."—*Standard.*

" A book on field sports and the best means of enjoying them is sometimes as repulsive and dry reading as a work on geometry.   Mr. Berkeley here gives an autobiography as much as a handbook of sports, and intersperses the details of hunting, riding to hounds, and other rural pastimes, with so much light and interesting matter that he has provided a consolidated fund of enjoyment for all who take an interest in any branch of rural life.........
It is certainly impossible to rise from any examination, long or short, of the author's lucubrations without becoming a better sportsman and a more experienced lover of the art than when the book was first opened."—*Morning Post.*

" It would be difficult to find two volumes containing more acute sense and ridiculous nonsense, more pleasant feeling and taste, more interesting anecdotes of birds, beasts, and fishes, or more absurd arguments, than this work of Mr. Berkeley's.   There is a vivacity and a freshness from beginning to end that are very delightful.........One of the pleasures of this work also consists in this, that you do not get anecdotes of fox-hunting alone, or shooting or fishing, or an other single sport, but of every one of these. Thus the reader is not wearied by stories of one kind, and therefore no want of freshness is found, which is too often the case in books which touch upon one portion of natural history or sport.   There is this further advantage, that in comparing the qualities of different creatures, you are enabled to compare the instinct of the horse and the dog, not only the instinct of one dog with that of another......It is sure to interest lovers of animals, and it shows something of the gentle and poetical side of sportsmen."—*Spectator.*

Samuel Tinsley, 10, Southampton Street, Strand.